BROKEN

THE BILLION HEIRS
BOOK 3

VANESSA VALE

HELEN HARDT

Broken by Helen Hardt and Vanessa Vale

Copyright © 2022 by Bridger Media and Helen Hardt, LLC

This is a work of fiction. Names, characters, places and incidents are the products of the author's imagination and used fictitiously. Any resemblance to actual persons, living or dead, businesses, companies, events or locales is entirely coincidental.

All rights reserved.

No part of this book may be reproduced in any form or by any electronic or mechanical means, including information storage and retrieval systems, without written permission from both authors, except for the use of brief quotations in a book review.

Cover design: Bridger Media

Cover graphic: Deposit Photos: SimpleLine, Scrudje, deniskrivoy.pho-to.gmail.com

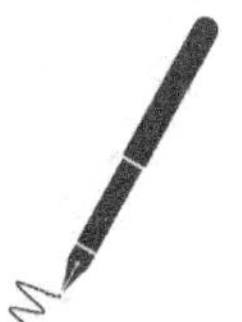

HANCE

LOVE.

I only loved one woman in my life, and that was nearly fifteen years ago.

Sure, I have my fun. I pick up a lady at The Dusty Rose now and again, maybe even take her out a time or two.

But that's it. I've only felt that spark once, and I've never found it since.

So I stopped thinking about love. Bachelorhood isn't so bad. I love the land, the animals, the work around the ranch. Hell, I even love my new brothers.

Damn it, though, the two of them brought romantic

love into the house. Within weeks. They had no trouble finding it right here in Bayfield, my hometown. To be fair, they didn't actually *find* love. Love seemed to find *them*. But love never found me, not in fifteen years.

Granted, I haven't exactly been looking, and life has been a fucking tornado since my father's death. I'm still a person of interest in the death of Joey Hopkins. I'm innocent, and I'm pretty sure the information Sadie uncovered will go a long way in proving it, but still...

It all gets to a guy after a while.

"I need to ride like the wind, boy," I say to Raphael, my midnight-black quarter horse, as I groom his flank with the curry comb.

I'm on my own at the ranch today. Miles is taking care of Sadie, who needs some serious time off. After what she's been through, fuck. I haven't seen them and don't plan to. They haven't left his bedroom as far as I know. Austin has gone with Carly to her therapy session in Billings.

So I'm taking the morning off too. Just Raphael and me and the sunshine.

I need an escape.

Ivory, a gorgeous cremello mare, snorts in the next stall. She's the horse Carly was grooming when Austin first laid eyes on her. He's told me the story a hundred times if he's told me once—how he was a goner the first time he saw her.

Miles says the same thing about Sadie. As soon as she sauntered up to him in that bar and asked him to take her panties, he was all in. Doesn't sound much like a love story, but the look in Miles's eyes when he tells it removes all doubt.

Maybe I should go over to that bar sometime.

"What do you think, buddy?" I brush a tangle out of Raphael's mane. "You think there's a woman out there for me?"

"I'd like to think there is."

That voice—melodic with just a touch of sexy rasp.

I drop the curry comb, and it lands on the hay-covered dirt with a thud.

I turn.

Standing in the door to the stable is a mirage.

A mirage from fifteen years ago.

It can't be. It just can't.

"Avery? Avery Marsh?"

"Hello, Chance."

God damn.

She was just in my thoughts.

One woman. I've loved only one woman in my life. People called it puppy love because we were seniors in high school, but I knew the truth. I knew what I felt was special.

My heart shattered when she left. She and her mother moved away a few months before our high school graduation, and I never heard from her again.

Not once.

But here she stands.

I know the stable stinks of hay and horse manure, but I swear to God, all I smell is the sweet citrus floral of Avery's perfume. She always smelled so good.

"I can't believe it's you." I blink to confirm it's really her.

"I'm actually here on..." She looks down at her feet.

Her blond hair is pulled up into a loose bun, and she's wearing black pants, a white silky blouse, and a dark red blazer.

But I see her in cut-off shorts and a violet tank top, her silky wheat-colored waves tumbling over her shoulders.

That's what she was wearing the last time we saw each other.

Those were the clothes she put back on after we made love in that spring on the edge of the ranch. We took each other's virginity that day, and the next day she left.

"Here on what?" I ask.

"On business, Chance." She draws in a breath as she

flips open a small black case to reveal a badge. "I'm a special agent with the FBI."

What? I never imagined her going into law enforcement, or her being back.

My eyes widen. "What? The EPA—"

"The EPA is doing its own investigation. I'm here about the death of Joseph Hopkins."

I shake my head. "I don't understand. We've been working with the local sheriff's office."

"Not anymore." She closes her badge holder. "As of now, the Feds are taking over this investigation. That means I'm here on Bridger Ranch until further notice."

1

VERY

My heart is racing, and my flesh is on fire.

Chance.

Chance Bridger.

I'm standing in front of Chance Bridger—the man who broke my heart fifteen years ago.

You think there's a woman out there for me?

I'd like to think there is.

What was I thinking, answering him like that?

I knew he was single. That he'd never left the ranch. I'm in the FBI and have access to all the intel I want on him. Except I hadn't looked into him until my supervisor put me on the case. To do so would have been too painful.

McGuinness knew the case was in my hometown. What he didn't know was that I'd been in a relationship with the suspect...and more.

One look at Chance and I'm that eighteen-year-old girl again, believing his professions of love and devotion, giving him the gift I could only give once. Trusting him. Loving him.

God, after all these years, the wound still hasn't healed. I didn't want to come back, but this is my job, and my hometown. I'm the best person for the case.

I'm a trained special agent for the FBI, so I know how to keep my emotions in check. No way can he have any idea how much I'm quaking inside at this moment, how my legs are jelly and I'm forcing them to stand.

How amazing he looks. Older. Bigger. He was big at eighteen, but now? Broad shoulders, barrel chest, the same chiseled jaw, and piercing eyes. He's even more handsome now than he was back then, which I didn't think was possible.

"You?" Chance shakes his head, his blue eyes boring into me. "Avery. I can't fucking believe it."

I solidify my stance. "Believe it. I just got back from Detective Peterson's office. He wasn't happy that we're taking the reins, but he'll deal."

"He's a dick," Chance mutters. He runs a hand over the back of his neck.

So are you.

I want to say the words so badly. I want to cry and scream and shout about how he shattered my heart all those years ago. I want answers, damn it. I *deserve* answers. He left me broken. So broken. And alone when I needed him the most.

But I maintain my professional countenance like a heavy winter coat because I don't have a choice. He hurt me once. I'll work this case and nothing more. I'll move on, just like I did before. But I have my eyes wide open now. I know what Chance is really like and I will protect my heart.

I shrug, playing nonchalant. "Locals are never happy when the Feds take over. We're used to it."

He doesn't reply. Just continues to stare at me, rake his gaze over every part of my body as if cataloging. And damn... It's like fifteen years have vanished in the blink of an eye. Chance Bridger can still melt me into a puddle with a look. Just like he did in the halls at school.

He's as gorgeous as ever, with that light auburn hair, fair skin, and blue eyes that I swear can see into my soul. The years have been kind to him. Other than a few laugh lines, his face still looks the same—russet scruff, sculpted jawline, full pink lips.

God, those lips...

And his body... He was always tall and muscular, but I swear he's broadened. He's wearing jeans and a red and black plaid shirt, and he's downright brawny.

I draw in a breath, regaining control over my body.

He shakes his head and takes a step toward me. "Damn, Avery, I have so many questions."

I hold up my hand. "I think you'd better leave the questions to me." I shove my badge into the purse hanging over my shoulder. "I have every intention of getting to the bottom of this murder."

His eyes widen and he takes a second. "You can't possibly believe that I—"

With a shake of my head, I push on. "I'm not here to believe anything, Chance. I'm here to investigate. I find facts. Sometimes, it turns out people aren't what I thought."

Yeah, it was a not-so-subtle dig.

He takes another tentative step toward me.

I draw in another breath.

His gaze meets mine and then drops to my lips, my chest. "Avery. My God. Where have you been?"

I cock my head. "I could ask you the same thing."

"You know where I've been." He raises his arms and then slaps his thighs. "Here. Working the ranch. And still wondering, after all these years, what the hell happened between us."

Really? He's going to play *that* card?

I'm not sure how to respond and still remain professional, but I don't have to because he keeps talking.

"You married?" he asks.

"Engaged," I say.

Why? Why did I just lie to him? I'm thirty-two years old, and I'm playing high school games. I need to stop it now. *Right* now.

I clear my throat. "That's a lie. I'm not engaged."

A little frown forms in his brow. "Oh?"

"I *was* engaged, but we broke it off a few months ago. I guess I'm still on auto-pilot with that answer."

There. At least that's the truth. Although my breakup with Tyler was nine months ago. Does that still count as only "a *few* months?" Close enough.

"Thank God," he murmurs.

"How about you?" I ask, even though I know the answer. Besides, he's not wearing a wedding ring, but that doesn't mean much working on a ranch. "Married? Engaged?"

"Hell no."

Even though I knew, a wave of relief sweeps through me when he says the words, and I berate myself for it. Chance doesn't want me. He never did. He ended things abruptly all those years ago—the fucking day after I gave myself to him.

He was just like every other high school boy—only after one thing.

Some lessons are learned the hard way.

I gave him my virginity—something I can never get back. All these years later, though, I still don't regret it. How can I? I've never found another man I wanted to give it to. Good thing, since I no longer have it to give.

He dumped me in a letter. A fucking letter!

And I still don't regret it.

That's how much I loved this man fifteen years ago. And looking at him now? The feelings inside me are whipping back around like a boomerang.

And I remember.

I remember that day at the spring...

Chance and I stand, facing each other, the whooshing of the waterfall splashing over the gray rock surrounding us like a protective bubble. He's so tall, so full of muscle, and I love the scattering of chestnut hair across his powerful pecs. How can he be so much a man at eighteen?

Ranch work, he's said so many times.

But still, I'm amazed.

This isn't the first time we've seen each other naked. We've gone nearly all the way on many occasions, but this time...

This time...we're going to do it.

We're going to make love.

We talked about waiting until prom night, but we decided yesterday that today will be the day. Here, by our spring.

The spring is on the edge of the Bridger property, and Chance swears no one else knows it's here. It's become our special spot, our magical place, and in my soul I almost feel like it's ethereal, and that the tiny evergreens sprouting through the cracks in the rock belong to fairies.

Chance reaches toward me, trails a finger down my cheek, my shoulder, over the top of my breasts. "You're so beautiful, Ave. You look like a goddess. A goddess of this spring."

I close my eyes, breathe in the robust scent of the fresh air laced with wildflowers and moss. Then I open them, meet his burning gaze.

"Are you sure?" he asks.

"I'm very sure." I smile.

I am. I ache for him, and when he touches me, he'll know how eager I am.

In fact, I've never been surer of anything in my life.

"Part of me wants to wait," he says, his heated gaze a contrast to his words. "Wait until we're husband and wife. But there's one part of me in particular that's done waiting."

Indeed, his cock is big and hard and majestic. I've seen it before. Handled it, sucked it.

But today, it will go inside me, and we'll be together in the most intimate way.

He slides his hands between my legs. "Mmm. Ready for me."

I whimper at his touch, roll my hips for more. "Always, Chance. I'll always be ready for you."

With his other hand, he takes mine, entwines our fingers together. "I love you so much, Avery Marsh."

"And I love you, Chance Bridger."

He leans down, brushes his lips over mine in a soft kiss, and then he leads me into the warm spring. It's not a bed. Far from it. But he takes me to a flat piece of rock and places me upon it. The height is perfect for him to slide inside me.

He leans down and takes my lips, kissing me deeply, passionately. Chance Bridger is an amazing kisser, and I love the way his soft tongue encircles mine. The kiss becomes hungrier, more raw, more untamed, and he squeezes one breast, thumbing my hard nipple.

I'm throbbing between my legs, so aching and empty...and today, I'll be filled.

Filled for the first time.

We've been waiting for a month. I went on the pill four weeks ago, and we had to wait for it to take effect.

And now?

We're both so needy and aching and full of the lust of young love.

Chance breaks the kiss and inhales a deep breath. "You sure, Ave?" he asks again.

I love that he's checking on me, but he doesn't need to.

"God, yes. I'm sure."

His body is tense while his words are gentle. "I don't want to hurt you."

I shake my head. "You won't."

"Put your arms around me, baby. I'm going to go in quickly, okay?"

"Please," I breathe.

I gasp as he pushes into me, taking my virginity with one swift thrust. Is there pain? A little. But it's nothing compared to the fulfillment I feel in my body, heart, and soul.

"Fuck," he growls, holding himself still deep inside me.

This is the man I love. The man who will be my husband. The man who will father my children.

The man who is my life.

"Okay?" He looks down into my eyes.

I shift my hips, adjusting to being stretched. I nod and raise my knees to squeeze his hips.

"Please," I beg.

He moves, pulls back, fills me again. "Fuck, kitten, you're so perfect. Tight. Too good."

He reaches between us and thumbs my clit. He's made me come before, but this is different. More sensation. Just more.

He moves and circles me. I lift up to meet him and we find a rhythm. We're not good at this, but it feels amazing. He clenches my hip with his large hand.

"Can you come?" His voice is rough.

I nod and wrap my legs around him, hooking my heels.

"Harder."

He listens and is soon pounding into me. It's too much. I cry out, clenching around him.

"Avery!" He thrusts deep and holds still.

I feel him fill me. Know I'm now his.

2

HANCE

SHE STARES at the stable behind her, gaze unfocused, as if she's thinking of something. I wonder if her thoughts match mine.

Of us, together, that first—and last—time.

I clear my throat and she blinks. Stiffens.

Blushes.

Yeah, the same thoughts. I remember her beneath me, the look on her face as I filled her for the first time. Claimed her, inside and out.

Her arms go over her chest. "I'll be around along with two other agents. We'll be heading to where the body was found, but that'll be a quick trip. The rest of the time we'll be digging through phone logs, bank records. Everything of your father's."

I nod.

"And yours," she adds.

"You can't—" I begin.

I don't want to start this entire insanity over again. Didn't Peterson already search through all the files?

Peterson. I have to admit, knowing that fucker was one-upped feels good.

She raises a hand. "Warrants and all the legal paperwork needed to learn about everything except your last colonoscopy is with your lawyer. Shankle, I think his name is."

Well fuck.

I nod.

She spins and turns the way she came, out the open stable door. "See you around."

"Kitten, wait," I call.

Fuck. I didn't mean for her pet name to slip out. I can't even remember why I began calling her that all those years ago.

She freezes and looks at me over her shoulder. "I'm not your *kitten.* I never was."

"You can't think that."

Her gaze narrows and she says nothing as she leaves. Literally walks off. Again.

This time, I know she's not going far. There's a murder to solve and somehow, in some way, it is now hers to solve.

———

"ARE YOU SHITTING ME?" Miles rubs a hand over his face.

I didn't go for that ride after all, but instead headed back into the house to get more coffee. Miles is in the kitchen in just a pair of jeans. I don't know where Sadie is and I don't ask.

I just told him about Avery. Our past.

"I didn't even know you had a girl."

"I don't," I reply. "I did. Then I didn't."

He tips his chin down and eyes me. For half-brothers, we don't look much alike. He's blond and smaller than I am, although not small at all.

"What the hell does that mean?" he asks.

I take a sip of coffee, lean against the counter. "We were hot and heavy. In love."

He looks at me as if I told him I dated an alien. "Love? At seventeen?"

"Eighteen. And absolutely," I say with complete certainty. "One day we're together"—I don't explain what *together* actually means—"and the next day, I find out from a neighbor in their trailer park that they up and moved to Phoenix."

"You never heard from her again?"

I shake my head. "Not once."

"Fuck. I didn't have a girl I loved back then, but I remember that age. It sucked *without* being dumped."

I glare. He shrugs.

"So she's back. Start over," he says, as if it's simple.

"Start over?" I meet my brother's gaze. "She left without a word, without a backward glance. Without a goodbye. Hell, without an explanation. I want that. I'll get that out of her while she's here. Maybe find closure."

He reaches in the fridge for the carton of eggs. "You still have a thing for her."

I look down at the counter. "Always have."

"No wonder you're such a cranky asshole all the time."

I can't help but smile at that. "Yeah. *That's* the reason. Not that our father was a bastard or that he's wrapped up, even in death, in illegal shit. Or that your girlfriend's brother was murdered on our ranch. Or any of the other shit going on right now."

"What you need is to get laid."

As if it's that simple. Hell, maybe for him it is. Sadie propositioned him in a bar, and now he's wearing love goggles.

I've slept with other women since Avery, but just for

release. That's what he means now, but seeing Avery, knowing she's here? On my ranch?

My heart wants her and her alone. So does my dick.

And that's a real fucking problem because she doesn't seem to want me in return.

"We'll go to the Dusty Rose tonight." Miles cracks six eggs into a cast iron skillet.

"Hungry much?" I ask.

"Hey, I'm making this for Sadie too. Where the hell is the bacon?"

I scratch my head. "I don't know. Louisa made breakfast four hours ago, dumbass, when you were still in bed. We do have work to do around here. Remember work?"

"Like I said, bro." Miles grinds some pepper over the frying eggs. "You need to get laid."

I shake my head. "Sex doesn't solve everything, Miles."

He gives me a sly grin. "It's a damned good start."

"How would lovely Sadie feel about you going with me to the Dusty Rose?"

He shrugs as if it's no big deal. Maybe it isn't. "She'll come along, of course. My girl can dance up a storm."

I roll my eyes. "No thanks."

"Suit yourself." He flicks the pan and flips all six eggs at once.

"Where'd you learn to do that?"

"When your mother's busy wooing husbands, you learn to fend for yourself." Miles pulls two plates out of the cupboard and grabs the bread that has popped out of the toaster. "Where's the butter?"

"Up your ass." I shake my head. "In the fridge, where it's been since you got here."

"Ha. You're funny. I'll say it a third time."

I hold up my hand to stop him. "I know. I need to get laid." I draw in a breath. Miles's eggs and toast smell good. Like home. "You know what? The Dusty Rose sounds like a plan. Better yet, what about that bar where you and Sadie met?"

"Not a bad alternative, but have you forgotten? It's ladies' night again at the Rose."

Ladies night—when the drinks are discounted and the pussy is plentiful.

I'll go. I'll go and tie one on.

But I won't end up in bed with anyone.

Not tonight. Not when Avery Marsh is mere miles away.

And not when I'm still fucking in love with her.

 VERY

I'M NOT sure how long I sat in my car before I finally turned on the ignition and drove away from Bridger Ranch.

It's crazy how much my body still reacts to Chance.

I never felt this with Tyler or anyone else.

I sigh. Tyler. Tyler Lipscomb is a wonderful man, and he was willing to take me with all my baggage. Until the day he wasn't.

You don't feel about me the way I feel about you, Avery.

I do, Ty.

You don't. You want to. Maybe you've even convinced yourself that you do, but you don't.

You're wrong. I love you.

I believe that, but not the way I love you. You love what I represent for you and your family. But you don't want me for me.

I wept as I removed the diamond solitaire from my left ring finger and placed it in the palm of his hand.

It was fruitless to argue further. He was right, and we both knew it.

I drive into Bayfield proper and stop at the local police station. They've allowed my partner, Roy Jarvis, and me to set up shop in an empty corner. The sheriff, Trevor Bryant, was very welcoming. Detective Mark Peterson? Not so much.

"Hey, partner," Jarvis says when I walk toward our small alcove. His sandy blond hair is covered by a black felt cowboy hat.

"Hey yourself. Trying to look the part?"

He grins. "When in Rome…" He makes some notes on his phone.

"Anyone tell you it's not cool to wear a hat inside? Especially in a lady's presence?"

He grins and removes the hat. Glances up. "Now look at me. I have hat head."

"Your own fault, city slicker. You can't pull that look off." I glance around. "They seem to be leaving you alone."

"You think? Other than Sheriff Bryant, no one's deigned to speak to me."

"The more things change... Locals always hate us." I take a seat across from Jarvis at our small table.

Documents are scattered every which way, and his laptop and tablet are both set up.

"You see him?" Jarvis asks.

My body warms. Damn it. "I did."

"And...?"

"And what?"

I haven't told Jarvis about my past with Chance Bridger. I don't want to get kicked off the case for a conflict of interest. It's too late. I should have told McGuinness when I got the assignment, but I didn't. If I mention it now, I'll look like an idiot.

It was his decision to put me on this assignment. He knows my past, knows I grew up here. He thinks it gives me an edge. A local, even though I haven't been one for over a decade. Still, I know the town. Know the people, or what I remember of them.

He knows I grew up in Bayfield, but not that I was a prime suspect's high school girlfriend. And more.

I'm a good agent and I'm not messing that up because of something that happened long ago. I can push my emotions to the side and do my job. And if Chance Bridger is a killer? Best I find out now.

Man, if anyone had told me back in high school that Chance Bridger had the capacity to kill a man, I'd have bet everything I owned—which at the time consisted of a stuffed bunny, a closet full of secondhand clothes, and a beat up old Chevelle—that they were wrong.

After I got that Dear Jane letter?

I'd have bet he could.

His words went beyond mean, beyond nasty. They were downright malignant.

And it was the day after...

The day after—

"Marsh?"

I jerk toward Jarvis's voice. Concern mars his brown eyes.

"You okay?"

"Yeah. Fine."

"Okay. You looked a little...freaked for a minute."

"Nope. Fine. Just a little weird being back." I switch topics. "The requisite warrants are in the hands of the Bridgers' attorney, Tom Shankle. I expect we'll have a shit ton of paperwork to pore through by morning."

"Morning?" Jarvis chuckles. "Are you kidding? No attorney worth his salt—especially one representing a billionaire—will go easy on us. I imagine we'll be fighting like mad dogs to get the information we need."

I don't reply. He's no doubt right. Most of the time, the subjects of our investigations are only too happy to comply with our requirements. The Feds scare the pants off most people. But Chance Bridger?

He doesn't scare easily, and I learned the hard way he's meaner than a rattler.

Though he didn't seem mean this morning... In the stable...

He seemed surprised to see me. Stunned.

Of course he would be. Only a masochist would return to that ranch after the caustic letter he sent me. I burned it on the road to Phoenix, but its contents are still branded in my mind.

It was fun, but it's over. You're good and all, but I can't keep you. You have to know that. I'm a Bridger and you're just another pussy I fucked at the spring.

I shake my head to clear the words out. I can't go there again. Not now. Not when I have a job to do. Not when he threw in my face what we did at the spring. That I gave myself to him and he left a piece of him behind.

Not that I'd ever tell him.

Chance might be tainted. Cruel.

But Grady isn't.

He's a teenager now, with auburn hair so like his father's.

Grady's my son. *Mine.* I'll either see Chance behind bars or in my rearview mirror. Because he'll never know about the child we made.

He won't get a chance to take anything else from me.

4

HANCE

It's been three days since Avery came to the ranch. The woman I remember was barely eighteen, but that quick visit pulled her out of adolescence to what she is now. Thirty-two.

She's filled out, gained womanly curves I don't remember. She still wears her hair long. The same tilt to her eyes. The curve of her cheekbones. The little scar above her right eyebrow.

I remember every inch of her, but a new version fills my mind. I could go to the police station and ask after her. Track her down to...

To what?

She didn't want me then and doesn't want me now.

I sigh, pulling a shirt off a hanger in my walk-in closet. The doorbell rings, soft in the distance, and I do up the buttons as I make my way to answer it. Austin and Carly are out and I haven't seen Miles.

It's after nine, but I've been up and out by six with the usual chores. This morning, a water pipe came loose in the stable and sprayed water in all directions outside the back doors. I came in to change while one of the ranch hands went to town to pick up new copper piping.

Louisa answers the door and lets Shankle, the family lawyer, in, accompanied by a man I don't recognize. She nods to me and heads back to the kitchen where the start of some meal smells good.

I shake Shankle's hand.

"Chance, this is Roy Jarvis, FBI."

I nod and offer my hand to him as well. He's in his forties with blond hair trimmed short and the pale complexion of someone who spends too much time indoors. He stands in front of the unlit fireplace, glances around the den. It's the room closest to the front door.

"Nice to meet you," he says. "I'm from the Phoenix office with my partner, Avery Marsh, who I believe you met the other day."

"Yes," I confirm, not wanting to share anything else.

While partners are often close, I don't think Avery would tell him about a high-school boyfriend.

Who cares?

"We've been working closely with your lawyer." Jarvis shifts his gaze to Shankle in a way that indicates *closely* means *with difficulty*, "He now has the warrants and other legal papers that allow us access to everything we need from the Bridgers. That includes yourself and your father, Jonathan Bridger."

I glance down at my shirt which is still untucked. "You're welcome to join me in my closet if you wish to check out my clothes. I was in there changing shirts."

He holds up a hand. "Avery is at Bridger Corp now, gathering more intel."

The main office is in Billings, which means I won't be seeing Avery today. Or anytime soon, I expect.

Jarvis scans the knickknacks on the mantel and picks up a framed photo of me on a horse when I was a kid. My mom put it there years ago and I haven't thought about it since.

"On what? The EPA investigation?" I ask.

He gives me a fake smile. "We'll work closely with them on our findings."

I glance at Shankle. He must be comfortable with what was asked of us to allow the access, but I have nothing to hide personally. "If you find that my father was breaking the law, I look forward to hearing your findings. I have nothing to hide. I haven't done anything wrong, so if Shankle's cleared you, go forth and search for what you like."

"I appreciate that."

His gaze roves over my face, quietly studying me. "You're not concerned about your assets being frozen?"

I shrug. "It's a pain in the ass having the government bothering us, but I don't hold out for the luxuries in life."

"This ranch isn't a homesteader's shack. And you have a private plane," he counters.

"The corporation has one," I reply. "I've only flown on it once, a few weeks ago when Austin's mother fell and we needed to get to her quickly. As for this house, my grandfather built it. I work the land, this property. I'm a rancher. I've never been involved in Bridger Corp. That was my father's business. Literally. My life is not, nor will it be, impacted by the loss of the Bridger money."

"That's why your brothers are here, though," he says. "To inherit."

As if I don't know that..

"Would you spend a year on this ranch for a billion dollars, Jarvis?"

He chuckles. "Sure would. Point taken."

"You're here for a reason," I say. "You wouldn't come all this way just to introduce yourself."

"I'm working the Joseph Hopkins murder."

"Good. I know Miles will be happy to update Sadie as to the latest on her brother's death."

He nods.

"The reason for us being here is for me to tell you I've approved their access," Shankle says. "And for him to meet you."

"I'll be here," I tell Jarvis. "Want to join me in deworming?"

Both men cringe as I expect.

"We'll let you get to it." Jarvis eyes me once more and then steps out onto the porch. "See you around, Bridger."

5

AVERY

I PICK up my buzzing phone. It's Jarvis.

"Hey," I say.

I spent the day in Billings making requests for papers and electronic data. I stayed long enough to receive two boxes of records and a promise that more would be in my email by the end of the day.

I'm now back at the little table in the police station in Bayfield, the surface covered in papers.

"You grew up here," Jarvis says.

"Yes."

"But you moved to Phoenix."

"Yes, when I was eighteen," I tell him.

"Did you know Chance Bridger?"

"I did. But not well," I reply.

I don't consider the words a lie. I *thought* I knew him well. Trusted him. Believed in him.

"Hmm," he says.

"What's up?" I scan the papers and try to organize them into piles.

"How old's Grady?"

My hands still. "Fourteen."

"Huh."

A chill races down my spine...and it's not from the freezing-ass air conditioning in this place.

"What?"

"Met Chance Bridger today. He's a handsome man."

"Great, you should date him."

He laughs. "By your tone, it sounds like you don't like him."

"I don't. He's an asshole."

In my job, I'm always direct, but this comment seems to surprise him.

"Always been one?"

"Always." Because he lied to me every second we were together. What I thought was real and genuine was a ploy to get into my pants. He said I was his first. What a crock.

"So you think he's into illegal chemical disposal like his old man?"

We pretty much have Jonathan Bridger for interstate crimes, even though he's dead and we can't put him behind bars, but nothing indicates that Chance was, or *is*, involved.

"No. I'm saying he's an asshole."

I'm not sharing more. No way. Being back here makes me nervous that my biggest secret—literally the biggest since Grady's close to six feet tall at only fourteen—will get out. Get back to Chance.

"Are you headed back here? I could use another set of eyes on all this paperwork." What an understatement.

"Yeah, I'll be there in ten."

I put my phone down and stare absently at the papers. Does Jarvis suspect Chance is Grady's father? They look a lot alike. I confirmed that when we were face to face once again the other day. I knew when he was born that he took after him, and as he grew, it was obvious he looked like a Bridger. But Grady and Chance now? Clearly son and father.

It doesn't matter. If Jarvis asks, I can lie. McGuinness sent me here specifically because I'm from Bayfield. He's smart and knows that people know each other's business in a small town like this. Chance and I are the same age. McGuiness didn't keep me from the investigation because of any possible connection. In fact, I think he did the opposite. The more inside intel we have on the Bridgers, the better.

Although I don't think he imagined sharing DNA with Chance counts.

I let out a heavy sigh.

Work. I'll focus on work. And if I can take down Chance Bridger in the process? Not a bad day.

My phone buzzes again, a number I don't recognize.

"Marsh," I say.

"Ms. Marsh, this is Dr. Nolan Hayes from forensics. I've got some news you're going to want to hear."

"Yeah? What have you got?"

"We took another look at the coroner's report on the body of Joseph Hopkins and found a few things."

My heart thuds. "Like what?"

"First of all, the autopsy was performed by the county coroner, not a medical examiner."

"Huh? On what planet does that make sense?"

"It's not uncommon," Dr. Hayes continues, "in rural areas for coroners to perform an autopsy, but because the coroner in this case isn't a medical doctor, we decided to take a second look."

"And?"

"We were able to extract some viable DNA from beneath the victim's fingernails."

I raise my eyebrows. "Seriously? That could be a major clue."

"Absolutely. First we're checking to make sure it doesn't belong to the victim himself, though I doubt that's the case because the body doesn't show any signs of deep scratches. So once we rule that out, it's probable that the DNA belongs to his killer."

"When will you know?" This is a great lead.

"I've put a rush on it, but DNA results, at the quickest, take about two business days."

I draw in a breath. "All right. So if you find out it's not the victim's, which it probably isn't, we need to get Chance Bridger's DNA."

"Right. He'll have to submit to a DNA test."

"Which he won't do quietly," I grumble. "We'll probably have to get a judge to order it."

Except...I *have* Chance's DNA. Half of it, anyway. I can get it from Grady.

Jarvis arrives, sitting down across from me and lifting his eyebrows.

"Anything else, Doctor?" I ask.

"Toxicology came back negative, which I expected given the age of the body, but there was something else remarkable as well."

"Yeah?"

"The victim is missing a portion of his liver."

"What?"

"Yeah. Is there any chance he donated part of his liver to a relative before his death?'

"I don't have a clue."

"The original report indicated the scar from surgery, but nothing else. I've looked at his medical records, and there's no mention of him donating for a transplant. But part of his liver is definitely gone, which means he donated pretty recently before he died. The liver will usually regenerate to its normal size within six to eight weeks after donation. Four months at max."

"Wow. So he donated part of his liver to someone."

"Yeah, usually to a relative, but I suppose he could have donated to anyone else who was a match."

Jarvis raises his eyebrows at me. I must have a mystified look on my face. Admittedly, this is strange.

"This may have nothing to do with his death, though," I say.

"Right," Dr. Hayes agrees, "but it's worthy of note."

"For sure." I clear my throat. "Let me know on the DNA as soon as you hear."

"I will. Talk to you later."

I end the call.

"You look like you just drank some bad wine," Jarvis says.

I shake my head. "That was Dr. Hayes from forensics. He got some DNA from under the victim's fingernails."

He smiles and shares the same satisfaction as I feel about this possible lead. "Great! That could be a big help."

"Yeah. I just have to get Chance Bridger to give us his DNA." I roll my eyes. "No problem."

"While he's a prime suspect, we haven't ruled out others who work at Bridger Ranch. Even those who worked at the trucking company with the victim."

"I agree. Although we won't get warrants for others' DNA without good reason, meaning we have to connect people to the case besides being co-workers or working where the body was found. Chance Bridger's the only one at the top of the list."

"When I saw him this morning," Jarvis says. "He indicated he'd cooperate. I think he just wants this over with."

My heart flutters, but I quickly shove that shit down. "You saw him this morning?"

"Yeah. I told you I was going over there with his attorney."

"Right." I sigh. "My mind is...a mess. Sorry. Didn't sleep well last night. That hotel bed sucks."

The hotel bed does suck, but I slept fine. I grew up sleeping on two chairs pushed together. Any mattress is a boon. The truth is that my mind is a mess. Just being around Chance Bridger again has me twisted in knots.

"Sorry to hear that. Everything okay?"

"Yeah. I'm good."

"I have to tell you, Marsh. While he's the son of Jonathan Bridger, had as much access to Bridger Corp as his father, I don't think Chance Bridger had anything to do with this murder. I mean, would he tell me I could look at anything I wanted if he was hiding something?"

I shrug. "Maybe. If he's got it so well hidden that no one could possibly ferret it out."

He scrunches up the side of his face in a weird look of doubt. "I just don't get that feeling."

"Whatever." I sigh. "Hayes is sending the DNA out to make sure it doesn't belong to the victim himself. Or maybe we'll get a hit in the system. Either way, he also found something else, though I doubt it has any bearing on the case."

"What?"

"Apparently the victim was a live liver donor. Part of his liver was removed."

"What makes you think he was a *live* donor?" Jarvis asks.

I gulp. "You mean..."

"Organ trafficking," Jarvis says.

"That's not what we're here to investigate," I say.

"Besides, the medical examiner said the scar was there at death, meaning it wasn't removed postmortem. The killer would have had to have kept him alive to perform the surgery. No one wants a non-working liver if they're organ traffickers. Besides, if all they wanted him for was the liver, then why suture him back up? Why not let him die on the table, then dump him?

He pauses, thinks it through, which is a lot. "Who the hell knows, but it's something to think about."

I don't buy this idea, but I want to get my partner's take. "You think this poor guy was killed for his liver?"

He shakes his head. "Hell, no. He was killed because he knew too much about Racehorse Hauling and Jonathan Bridger, and he had to go. But if someone needed a liver...and Joey Hopkins had one..."

"There's no evidence Bridger was into that," I say. The medical examiner's news is the first hint of anything like organ trafficking we've seen in our investigation. Same goes for Peterson's work before us.

"True. But it might be a good idea to see if the victim has any living relatives who have, or had, liver disease."

I glance through my notes on the victim. "His father, Curt Hopkins, is an alcoholic—a prime candidate for liver disease. He held his only daughter at gunpoint a week ago. He's in prison."

"We'll need his medical records," Jarvis says. "I'm on it."

Then I drop my jaw as something in the report catches my eye.

"And that daughter? She's the significant other of Miles Bridger, Chance's half brother."

6

HANCE

"COME WITH US," Carly says. "It's just dinner out. Austin already gave Louisa the night off."

"Without asking me first," I growl.

"I didn't realize we needed permission." Austin drapes his arms around Carly's shoulders. "Miles and Sadie are meeting us there. It's the chophouse over on County Road Nine. Nothing fancy, but the ladies deserve a night out."

"I don't have a lady on my arm," I remind them. I instantly think of Avery, which is ridiculous.

"Maybe you'll find one there," Carly urges.

"At the chophouse?" I shake my head. "If no one at the

Dusty Rose caught my eye the other night, I doubt there's a chance at that place."

"There were plenty of gorgeous women at the Rose," Austin says. "And any one of them would have loved some attention from you. You were the one who wasn't looking."

I sigh. "When you're right, you're right."

Austin shakes his head. "You need to get over this FBI chick. It's been fifteen years, man. Let it go."

"I just want to know why." I thread my fingers through my hair. "One day we were in love, and the next day, she's gone. I don't get it. I don't get any of it."

"You want some closure." Carly gives me a small smile of reassurance. "That's understandable."

I nod, but truth be told, I want a hell of a lot more than closure from Avery Marsh.

One look at her, and fifteen years faded away in an instant.

I still want her.

I still love her.

Fuck.

"You still have to eat, Chance," Austin reminds me.

I grab my hat off the peg by the door. "Fine. I'll go."

———

SITTING in a chair at the end of a wooden booth with my brothers and their two ladies doesn't make me a fifth wheel at all. I roll my eyes. Every time a server walks by, I get bumped.

"Why the hell didn't they give us one of those round tables?" I grumble.

"Let's ask them to change," Sadie says. "It shouldn't be any trouble."

"Are you kidding me?" I roll my eyes. "This place is packed."

Another whomp to the back of my head.

"Sorry, sir," a server says with a smile. "I'm Amy and I'll be taking care of you tonight. Can I start you with anything to drink?"

"God, yes," I say. "Whatever you've got on tap, as long as it's cold and frothy." Then I feel like a heel for not allowing the ladies to order first. "Sorry," I mumble.

"I'll have a glass of Chardonnay," Sadie says.

"Just mineral water." Carly smiles.

"For your beer, sir," Amy continues, "we have Budweiser, Coors Extra Gold, and Guinness."

"Guinness."

"Very good." She nods to Austin.

"I'll have a Guinness, too."

"And you?" To Miles.

"Scotch. Neat."

"Any particular brand?"

"The well brand is fine."

She nods as she uses a palm-held ordering device. "Perfect. Would you like to order an appetizer?"

God, can this ever end?

Carly and Sadie discuss the merits of calamari over shrimp cocktail while the hostess walks by with more patrons, jarring the back of my chair once more.

"Damn," I can't help mumbling, as I look over my shoulder.

My stomach plummets.

A man and a woman are settling into a booth—Avery Marsh and her partner, Roy Jarvis.

Of course, Avery takes the side of the booth that faces me. Maybe she senses I'm staring. Maybe it's because she's an FBI agent. Whatever the reason, she looks up and sees me.

Her eyes widen for a split second. Then they narrow. She's not happy to see me for sure, but damn...she looks like sex on a stick. Her blond hair is down now, flowing over her shoulders. Her lips are full and pink, and those blue eyes...

"Mozzarella sticks?"

I jolt at Sadie's voice. "What? Oh, whatever's fine with me."

I look at Avery again, who, after only being seated for less than a minute, stands and makes her way to the exit.

I follow with my eyes and seconds later I pop to my feet, cutting off people in the pathway. I ignore my newfound family and go after Avery.

I saw her once. For minutes. I have to know. I have to confront her. Because not seeing her but knowing she's in town is fucking killing me.

She's in the parking lot, walking down a row of cars. People are coming and going, but it's a lot less busy than inside.

"Avery!" I call.

She turns, crosses her arms over her chest.

"Hey, Chance." Her tone is indifferent, bordering on dismissive.

"Leaving again?"

She narrows her eyes. Does she get my double meaning? Probably.

"I haven't heard a word from you since I've been in town. Not surprising."

Her comeback is well aimed. I cross my arms so my stance matches hers.

"I thought you forgot about me." Again, double meaning.

"Are we talking about now or fifteen years ago?" she asks.

"You tell me."

She looks gorgeous, from her wedge-heeled sandals to her dress that looks like a long T-shirt to those gorgeous blond locks.

"You used to wear a shirt like that." My groin tightens. "Remember? It was mine."

She looks down at her blue dress. It's not revealing, but it showcases the curves of her breasts and hips. My dick stirs. Again. I remember the feel of her skin, the scent of her. The way her pussy was so fucking tight around me.

"I remember a lot of things."

"Like how we kissed?" I take a step closer.

Her eyes widen, but she doesn't retreat.

"Like how you used to climb in my lap and let me touch you? How you spread your legs for me at the spring?"

She jolts as if she stuck her finger in an outlet and takes off.

I follow, keeping up with her easily due to my long legs. I catch her, touch her upper arm, and spin her around.

I hate her for leaving. For leaving without any explanation. I love her though. I always have. Never have I better understood the thin line between love and hate.

The need in me to taste and remember what it was like between us is too strong to resist.

My father, the investigation, the murder—all of it disappears when my lips meet hers.

Fuck, she's just as I remember.

A gasp escapes her and I take the advantage and plunge my tongue into her mouth. She's sweet as I remember, lush and soft in my hold. And that scent... Some flower that is solely hers.

She's so much smaller than I am. I lift her, one hand banded low about her back, the other capturing the back of her head.

I lift my mouth to tilt my head.

"Chance," she whispers.

We're in a parking lot, and the irony of the moment isn't lost on me. If Austin comes out and finds me making out with the lead agent on the case, he'll be pissed, maybe even punch me like I did him when he was consumed by Carly.

I understand now. The need. The desire to claim.

I kiss along Avery's jaw to her ear. We're in plain sight, and I can't do what I want and bend her over the nearest car's hood.

"Is that pussy wet for me like it was at the spring?" I growl, my dick pressing into her so she knows I want her as much now as I did then.

She stiffens in my hold and pulls back, our breaths mingling. Her eyes flutter open and I get lost in hers for a moment. They're so blue. So fucking blue like the Montana summer sky.

"You asshole," she seethes.

"Me? Kitten, you're the one who left town."

"You're the one who told me I was a whore."

What?

I blink, set her on her feet. "I'd never say that about you."

She turns and practically runs across the lot. I make chase again. A car lock beeps and she flings open the passenger door of a black sedan, probably a rental.

"Leave me alone, Chance."

"No." My heart is beating as if I ran here from the ranch. "No fucking way."

"We have nothing to say to each other."

"Right. That's how you like it."

She reaches in, grabs a folder full of papers, and then stands inside the open door, eyeing me as if I were shit on her shoe.

"What do you want from me?" she demands. "I'm here to work the case and then I'll be gone."

"Just like the day after I made you mine."

She moves to close the door, but I'm blocking her escape since we're between two parked cars. She turns again and heads the other direction, through the next row.

"You don't have to say anything now. I got it all loud and clear in your letter. Fuck off, Chance!"

Two patrons leaving the restaurant eye me with contempt as Avery runs back inside, leaving me standing there. Stunned.

Confused.

"What letter?" I ask out loud.

But she's not there to answer.

7

VERY

INSTEAD OF GOING BACK to my table, I head straight for the ladies' room. I set the folder down and then grasp the porcelain edge of the sink and stare into the mirror. The whites of my eyes look hazy—hazy with the tears that are about to fall.

I sniff them back as best I can, grab a paper towel from the dispenser, and unceremoniously blow my nose into it. It's rough against my skin, but I don't care. Life is rough. Fucking rough.

A toilet flushes, and a pretty young woman with striking green eyes appears at the sink next to mine. She pumps some hand soap into her palms, turns on the faucet, and then glances over at me.

Her eyes widen. "Are you okay?"

"Fine. Thank you." I loosen my grip from the sink and take a longer look at her. She looks vaguely familiar to me.

"You sure?" she pushes. "You look a little...dazed... And sad."

Nothing gets by this woman. Her eyes are kind, though, and right now I can sure use some kindness. My partner's a nice guy, but it's not like I can dump my history on him. Especially when it's linked with the case. "My past recently collided with my present." I sniffle a bit. "I'll be fine. I just need a minute."

The woman grabs a couple paper towels from the dispenser, dries her hands, and tosses them into the waste receptacle between the sinks. "All right. It was nice to meet you anyway. My name's Carly." She holds out her hand. Then her eyes go wide in recognition. "Oh my God. Avery Marsh?"

I nod, then frown. "The one and only. Have we met?"

"I was two years behind you in high school," she explains. "You were supposed to be the prom queen, but then you and your mom disappeared."

Then I realize why she looks familiar. Sure, Bayfield's a small town, and I probably knew Carly back in high school, but I've largely erased those years from my mind. No. I recognize her because she was one of the women rescued from that billionaire's island that got shut down over a year ago. It was all over the news, and even though the women's names weren't made public, the FBI had access. I remember seeing that she was from Bayfield. I never let myself think about Bayfield, so I said a quick prayer for her wellbeing and never gave her another thought.

Until I got this case. Her name came up in the notes. She's involved with one of Chance's brothers—Austin. God, small-town life at its finest.

"Carly Vance," I say. "Your father's the mayor."

"Yeah, he is." She clears her throat. "I... Chance told us you were in town. When he ran out, I didn't get a good look at you. I had no idea the two of you were—"

"We weren't," I say succinctly.

"Oh. I'm sorry. I guess Chance is back at our table now."

I blink at her and roll my shoulders back. "I really don't know—or care—where Chance Bridger is."

My sharp tone makes her flinch.

"I'm sorry. I didn't mean to—"

I silence her with a hand gesture. "You don't need to apologize and I... It's rough being back. Austin Bridger may be a wonderful man. I have no idea. Chance Bridger, on the other hand?" I shake my head, again grabbing the edge of the sink. "Not so wonderful."

She doesn't reply.

She simply stares at me, her green eyes wide. Her lips twitch as if she wants to say something, but nothing comes.

"Nice to see you, Carly. Now if you'll excuse me." I grab the folder, whisk out of the bathroom, and head back to Jarvis.

I glance at the table where Chance was seated on the end. He's not there, but two handsome men—one dark, one blond—presumably his half-brothers, sit across from each other. A gorgeous and curvy dark-haired woman sits with them as well. Of course. She must be Sadie Hopkins, the brother of the victim in the murder I'm investigating.

My God, I've walked right into a family dynamic I never wanted.

All their eyes are trained on me as I make my way back to the table where Jarvis is perusing a menu. Yeah, they know there's something between Chance and me. No, not present tense. Past. They can tell we have a history because there is no *present* with us. None. Especially not after that parking lot conversation.

"What the hell was that all about?" he asks.

"We need to go." I loom over the table. I don't want to sit because we're not staying.

"I just got my drink." He picks up a lowball glass of what looks like bourbon or scotch. "And I ordered an appetizer."

I offer him a shrug. "Good enough. Then *I'm* leaving."

"Marsh…"

I ignore him and keep walking until I've reached the entrance once again. I have no idea where Chance is, but I can't risk running back into him in the parking lot once again. My rental car is there, but I can't take it anyway or Jarvis won't have a way to get back to the hotel. Since he drove, he has the keys.

Fuck it all.

I grab my phone and pull up the Uber app. Are there even any Uber drivers working this tiny town?

Thank God. There is a driver, and she's only ten minutes away. I schedule a ride and then walk around to the other side of the building where I can keep my eye on the main road while steering clear of the lot.

Time crawls. Ten minutes may as well be ten hours.

I draw in a deep breath—

"Kitten."

Damn, that voice. Deep and rich with just a touch of rasp. That voice that used to turn my legs into a quivering mess.

It still does.

Luckily I'm leaning against the building so I remain standing. I close my eyes. "Go away, Chance."

Then a spark as his finger touches my cheek.

I startle, open my eyes. "Please. Don't do this."

"You're going to have to tell me," he says.

"Tell you what? To leave me alone? I think I made that pretty clear. I don't owe you any explanation."

"You do, kitten." His voice is a deep rasp. Soft, missing that hard edge from just a few minutes ago. "You have to tell me why you left."

He can't be serious. He knows damned well why I left. "I don't have to do anything except figure out who murdered that poor guy on your ranch. That's it. And once I do that, I'm never setting foot in this town again."

"Please..."

My phone buzzes. "My ride is here."

I walk to the front of the restaurant and take a look at the blue Toyota Prius. I check the license plates against the app, and then I walk briskly toward the car and open the door to the back seat. "Are you Elaine?" I ask the middle-aged woman in the driver's seat.

"I sure am. You must be Avery."

"I am." I slide into the seat and attempt to shut the door, but—

Chance has hold of it, and he's stronger than I am.

My God, he was always so strong. Big and strong and protective...

"Avery. Don't."

"Let go of the door, Chance."

"Please. I'll drive you wherever you need to go. Just talk to me."

"Absolutely not." I summon every bit of strength I possess and yank the door closed. "Step on it," I say to Elaine.

———

THE NEXT MORNING, after checking in briefly with Jarvis, I head to Union Prison to speak to Curt Hopkins, the victim's father. After flashing my badge and surrendering my weapon, I'm led through security to talk to the captain of the guards, a burly older man who's bald as a cue ball.

"I understand you're with the FBI, ma'am," he says to me.

"Yes I am, Captain"—I eye his name tag —"Fitzpatrick."

"And you're interested in seeing Curt Hopkins?"

"Yes. He may have evidence that is relative to a case I'm working on. He's the father of the victim, Joseph Hopkins."

"Hopkins is on work duty right now in the laundry.

And visiting hours are on Tuesday and Thursday afternoons."

"I understand, but I'm not visiting. I'm not his girlfriend, I'm the FBI. I can speak to him whenever I want." I don't have time for a delay. I'm here and I'm going to talk to the guy. "I'm on a tight schedule. I'm sure the laundry facility can get along without Mr. Hopkins for a few moments. This is official FBI business."

Fitzpatrick's jaw goes rigid. "Let me check with the warden."

Red tape galore. I'm used to it. State-run prisons hate giving Feds any leeway at all. So I'll jump through their hoops. I'll do what I have to do to get this job done so I can get out of Montana and away from Chance Bridger—this time for good.

Yeah, that's all I've been thinking about since I left him at the restaurant the night before. Getting the hell out of Bayfield. It may be good for the case having me here, knowing all the players involved, but it wasn't good for me. I 'haven't been this twisted up since... since I got Chance's letter.

I'd thought I'd buried it all pretty well. Boy, I was fucking wrong.

Fitzpatrick walks out of earshot, his cell phone glued to his ear. He and the warden will exchange smack talk about the Feds, and then he'll come back to me and begrudgingly let me speak to the prisoner of my choice.

I know the drill.

Right on schedule, Fitzpatrick returns in about five minutes. "Follow me."

"Thank you, Captain."

A few moments later, I'm sitting in the visiting area behind a wall of glass.

And I wait...

8

———

HANCE

I DIDN'T SLEEP for shit. Dreams of Avery Marsh plagued me all night.

The letter.

What fucking letter was she talking about?

I never wrote her any letter. The day after we made love, she and her mother, Linda, disappeared, never to be heard from again.

Scuttlebutt in town was that Linda inherited some dough from a long lost aunt, and she packed Avery up and left.

But Avery had just turned eighteen. She could have

stayed. I'd have seen that she was taken care of. She loved me.

Or so I thought.

None of it made any sense, and I finished my senior year of high school in a numb-ass state and then, against my father's strict orders, skipped college and began to work fulltime on the ranch doing as much grunt work as I could find. Something about manual labor helped my headspace, and I worked harder than any of the hands, to the point where I earned their total respect. No longer was I the owner's rich spoiled brat. I was one of them.

I still am. That's why I make Austin and Miles do shit like mend fences and fix tractors, which Miles is really good at, given his knowledge of mechanics. Sure, we could let the hands do it all, but if I have to share my inheritance with two men I never knew existed, they're going to fucking earn it.

It was how I steered clear of my father too. He spent his time at the office, making deals, doing shit I knew nothing about. Looking back, maybe I should've kept tabs on what he was up to. We wouldn't be in this clusterfuck now. Then again, if I'd known, I'd probably be headed to jail right now.

I pour myself a cup of coffee when Miles walks into the kitchen.

"Hey, stranger," he says. "Where'd you take off to last night?"

I suppose I owe my brother an explanation for disappearing on them. "I walked around town for a while, went into the pool hall, and then hitched a ride home with one of the hands."

"Ah..." Miles pours some coffee for himself. "I've enjoyed the extra sleep, especially with Sadie in my bed, but that's a few days in a row now that you haven't roused Austin and me out of bed at the butt crack of dawn. Surely this woman isn't making you swear off work."

"Hell, no." I set my coffee down and stretch my arms above my head. "She's what made me swear *on* work fifteen years ago. Not that my father didn't make me earn my keep around here. But after Avery took off, I went all in. There's nothing I don't know how to do around here."

Miles takes a seat at the kitchen table and sips his coffee. "Apparently Carly ran into her in the bathroom last night. At the restaurant. She came back to the table and told us about it."

I stiffen. Then, "So?"

"So...Carly said she looked terrible. Very sad."

I try to ignore the spike that pierces my heart at the thought of Avery's sadness. Hell, why should I care? She left *me*. "Not my concern."

"Avery left after that," Miles says. "We saw her say something to her partner and then cut out."

I don't reply. I know very well where Avery went. She got into a car with some Uber driver and drove off. That's when I walked the half mile back into town and went to the pool hall.

"We tried to call you," he continues.

"Phone died." I take a swill of coffee, wince when it burns my tongue.

"The girls were worried, but Austin and I figured you could take care of yourself."

"Thanks for the vote of confidence." I scoff.

"You know what you need?" Miles asks.

I roll my eyes. "To get laid?"

He chuckles. "To be truthful, that wouldn't hurt, but I was thinking of something else."

"And what might that be?"

"You need to figure out why in hell this woman left you fifteen years ago, because from what I can ascertain, it wasn't her idea."

"How do you know that?"

He shrugs. "If you two were as hot as you say, then why is she back and upset?"

I have no fucking clue. "What does it matter? She was eighteen. She could have stayed."

"Eighteen is such an arbitrary damned age." Miles draws in a breath. "Hell, when I was eighteen, I thought I knew everything. It's amazing how much less I know now than then."

"And this has *what* to do with my situation?" I push, trying to figure out why he knows all about my love life—or lack thereof—and wants to give me advice.

"I'm just saying." He scratches the back of his neck and looks my way. "She was barely eighteen. Her mother was the one constant in her life. Don't blame her for not having the strength to venture out on her own. I mean, could she? Did she have the money? A support system—besides you—to stick around? Maybe she didn't have a choice if she wanted a roof over her head."

"She had me!" I snap. "Look, I would have understood if she had to leave. Hell, even if she *wanted* to leave, for that matter. But she should have told me. Fuck it all. Did she know that day at the spring?"

He looks at me, confused. "Day at the spring? What the fuck are you talking about?"

I sigh. He might have picked up slivers of info from me and 'Carly, but he doesn't know everything. I sure as shit don't kiss and tell. "Never mind." I set my empty coffee cup in the sink and walk back to my bedroom.

Time to stop feeling fucking sorry for myself. There's work to be done.

And once I've kicked my brothers' asses with manure shoveling? I'm going to head into town, find Avery Marsh, and make her talk to me.

9

VERY

TEN MINUTES PASS before a middle-aged man with dark hair and a beer belly is led to the small cubicle where I'm sitting.

He sits across from me behind the thick plexiglass and picks up the phone.

I do the same. "Mr. Hopkins," I say in my work voice, "I'm special agent Avery Marsh with the FBI. I have some questions about the murder of your son, Joseph Hopkins."

"I don't know shit about what happened to him. He was an ingrate, for sure."

Lovely. A deadbeat father.

I keep the look on my face non-committal. "An ingrate?"

"Yeah. He could have gone into business with me, and he chose not to."

"Your construction company?"

My research shows his business is in bad shape, though it once thrived when Hopkins was younger. What happened?

One look at him tells the tale. Alcohol. The man's in withdrawal, and it shows. Bloodshot eyes, swollen skin, red nose like Rudolph. I'm pretty sure this is where Joey Hopkins's missing liver went. No way Curt would have gotten a liver from anyone else without getting off the sauce for at least a year.

"Tell me your connection to Racehorse Hauling," I say.

"Don't know what you're talking about."

"According to your daughter's affidavit, she found an ashtray with the company's logo in your living room."

He rolls his eyes and leans back in his chair. "Rainey probably found it at a garage sale. Or Joey gave it to me. He worked for them."

"But you're maintaining you had no connection to Racehorse whatsoever?"

"That's exactly what I'm maintaining, lady."

"Special Agent Marsh," I correct him. "What was your connection to Jonathan Bridger?"

He cocks his head. "The rich fucker? Didn't know him."

"So you weren't aware that over a dozen corporations—all of which Jonathan Bridger held majority ownership in—contracted with Racehorse Hauling to transport hazardous chemicals across state lines and across the Canadian border for illegal disposal?"

"Do I look like I even know what a hazardous chemical is, la—"

I glare at him.

"—dy?"

I draw in a breath and count to ten. Or try to. I only make it to three.

He sure as hell *does* look like he knows what a hazardous chemical is. He is the personification of a hazardous chemical.

I try a different direction. "When's the last time you saw your son, Mr. Hopkins?"

A shrug pushes up the orange prison shirt. "He disappeared a couple years ago."

"So you had no contact with him prior to his death, which examiners estimate to have occurred about three to four months ago?"

"Why would I have contact with him?" His voice rises. "He was a shithead ingrate."

Ingrate. Again. Why am I even surprised? This is a

man who held his only daughter at gunpoint. That's why he's in prison.

Working for the FBI, I should be hardened to assholes. I've met enough of them.

"Do you know why a portion of your son's liver had been removed prior to his death?"

"What?" He widens his eyes.

Okay, maybe that liver isn't inside Curt Hopkins.

"Looks like your son was a live liver donor."

"I don't know shit about that." He shakes his head. "Who the hell would want his liver?"

Not a question I care to contemplate, so I move on.

"Mister—"

My phone buzzes in my purse. I pull it out.

Grady.

"Sorry. If you'll excuse me, I have to take this."

"Don't bother coming back, lady," he says into the phone. "I don't have any info for you."

"Oh, I'll be back." I nod to one of the guards. "I have to take a phone call."

The guard escorts me out of the visitation area to a hallway, and I quickly call Grady back.

"Hey, Mom," he says before the second ring.

"Hey, baby. Sorry I missed the call. I was in a meeting. You okay?" I wonder. He stays with my mother when I have to work, but this trip away is longer than most.

"Not really."

My heart drops. "What?"

"No. I mean I'm fine. Grandma made me call you. I got sent home from school today."

"Are you sick?"

"No. I'm fine. I've been...suspended."

For God's sake. Just what I need while I'm out of town on assignment. Investigating Grady's biological father, no less.

Grady's a good kid. He gets good grades, excels at sports, and volunteers with the homeless veterans during the summers. Why would my sweet son get suspended?

Whatever happened can't possibly be his fault. My frustration and anger from the quick talk with Hopkins is pushed onto whomever has messed with my son.

"Why?" I ask.

"I... Jeez, Mom, it was the first time. I swear."

My mind races. He's fine. He's not hurt. Nothing can be that bad. The first time for what? He's way too young to be thinking about...

Oh, God...

"Just tell me what you did, Grady." I try to keep my voice even.

"I had a joint in my backpack. It fell out during Algebra class, and the teacher saw it before I could grab it."

Pot? Okay.

I can handle pot.

He's not having sex at fourteen. It's okay. Since I was a teenage mother, I've always made subtle yet important statements about safe sex, using condoms and doing all the things in life before having a kid. Being stable. Having a job. A partner in life. Everything I *didn't* do.

"Where the hell did you get pot?" I yell. "You know how I feel about drugs. How Grandma feels about drugs."

"I told you," he replies. "It was the first time. I didn't even get a chance to smoke it."

"Why would you even *have* it?" I demand. "Drugs at school? Seriously?"

"It was stupid. Monty got three joints from his older brother, and he gave one to Luke and one to me."

"So you didn't smoke it."

"I swear to God, Mom."

"Were you going to?"

Silence.

Of course he was going to. He's fourteen, and he's curious. Fuck it all.

"Fine. So you're suspended, but that's just your school punishment. When I get home, we'll discuss your home punishment. And I hope they took the thing."

"Yeah, and I'm pretty sure Mr. Harvey is getting stoned right now."

I sigh. Grady's probably not wrong. His principal, Jonas Harvey, was a classmate of mine in college. He was a huge pothead. I never told Grady, but apparently it's not a secret.

"How long is the suspension?" I ask.

"Two days, including today."

"All right. Let me talk to Grandma, please. And Grady?"

"Yeah?"

"I love you."

"I love you too, Mom. And thanks for not going ballistic."

"Oh, I'm going ballistic," I tell him. "I'm just too far away for you to notice."

He doesn't reply and I hear some fumbling through the phone.

"Avery," my mother's voice comes soft and clear.

"Hey, Mom. I'm sorry you had to deal with this while I'm not there."

"He's a good boy," she says. "I feel certain this is a one-time thing."

"I hope you're right. I knew that Monty had a bad streak. I don't know why Grady and Luke took up with him. Imagine, giving weed to someone who's only fourteen."

"It's just growing pains, sweetie. He'll be all right."

"God, I hope so. He's everything to me, Mom."

"I know he is. To me as well."

I draw in a breath. "Mom, I need you to do me a favor."

"Of course."

"Go into Grady's room and find his comb and hairbrush. See if there are any hairs on them that have a viable root. It's that tiny white part at the end of the hair."

She's quiet for a moment. "Avery, what are you doing?"

"You know why I'm here," I tell her. "You're a smart woman. You know what I'm looking for. If you find what I need, overnight it to me at the hotel. The sooner the better."

"And how am I supposed to snoop through your son's things when he's home on suspension?"

I sigh. "I don't know. I suppose I could just have him do a cheek swab, but he'll ask why, and I made a promise to him long ago never to lie to him."

"Except you haven't kept that promise. You told him his father was dead."

"That's the one thing I lied about," I say. "And he *was* dead to me, Mom."

He was, for many years.

And now he's not. He's alive. Alive and big and strong and gorgeous and the amazing kisser he always was. It was... God. At first, I was surprised. But I shouldn't have been. Chance was always a little dominant, a little possessive, and he liked to kiss me, to touch me, to show me I belonged to him whenever we were together.

I loved it, the feeling of knowing I was his.

The recent kiss? The same. I felt like he was claiming me all over again. Hot and fierce. Demanding. Chance takes, but also gives. I crave—

"Avery..."

I practically fan myself remembering, which makes me cranky, because I shouldn't like what he did. I shouldn't want more. *Need* more.

"Just get the hair. Do it now, and make some excuse to go out and overnight it to me. There's still time for me to get it by morning."

"I'll try. But sweetheart, I need to talk to you about something. When you have some time."

"Is it urgent?"

A moment passes. Then, "No."

I'm too focused on this case, on Chance, on getting the hell away from those kisses to hear anything else right now. "Then it has to wait. Get the hair, and then please take care of my son until I'm home."

10

HANCE

I SHOULD FORGET AVERY. Just push her out of my mind and move on with my life. That has never worked. Not one fucking time in all these years. Now, she mentioned a letter.

A letter.

I can't get past it because I have no idea what she's talking about. I toss. Turn. Stare at the ceiling. Get up for the usual chores and make coffee.

Miles and Austin shuffle into the kitchen and grab mugs to fill with caffeine.

I stare as the coffee maker drips, drips, drips...

That's it. Right there. I can't take another second of not knowing. Of having Avery in town and not being near her. I need answers. I need them now.

I turn, cut across the kitchen. "You two are on your own this morning."

"Where the hell are you going?" Austin calls.

"To get the truth." I snag my hat off the hook by the mudroom.

The answer doesn't satisfy them and they keep at it, but I ignore everything they ask and head to my truck in the garage.

I drive into town, having no real memory of doing so, and pull up in front of the motel on the south side of town. It's the only one in Bayfield, so it's easy to know where Avery's staying.

It's early, just after six. The sun's up, but low in the sky. It's going to be a warm day. A pretty one. I don't give a shit about any of it except talking to Avery about this letter.

Fortunately, because Bayfield is small, I know the motel owner and have the room number out of her in thirty seconds. The woman's old enough to remember Avery and I were a thing in high school and that she hasn't been back since. Maybe she hopes for a reconciliation as much as I do.

Whatever, it doesn't matter.

I knock on room 102. Again.

The door slides open, the chain barring my entry to a sleepy and rumpled Avery.

"Let me in." While I have zero patience left at this point, I keep my voice soft. Gentle. The last thing I want to do is scare her or kick the door in. I don't want to hurt my chances of getting to the woman who has been mine since we were kids.

"What... What are you doing here?" She clears her throat.

Good. She can't escape the conversation we're going to have.

"Let me in, kitten."

Her eyes flare. "We don't have anything to talk about."

"I want to know about the letter, and I'm not doing it through a door."

She looks down and I finally do as well. She's in a sleep shirt and nothing else. While the hem of it comes to mid-thigh, longer than some dresses women wear these days, the look makes my dick twitch. She's got to be warm and soft from sleep and I wonder if she's wearing panties because she sure as hell isn't wearing a bra. Those little nipples I used to love to suck are hard and pointy beneath the thin cotton.

She glances around, as if she can see around me to the rest of the parking lot, and then sighs and closes the door enough to undo the chain.

She opens the door and steps back. I enter, and pitch black engulfs us when she closes the door behind me. I know we're closed in together. Her scent is heavy in the small room and one small whiff brings back every memory I have of us.

With a snick, the bedside lamp comes on. I turn to Avery, and her hand is on the switch on the wall.

I want to go to her, grab her, kiss her. Fuck the answers I want from her. But I don't. I may have gotten away with my mouth on hers the night before, but not now. Not the way she's glaring.

"The letter, kitten."

She curls her hands into fists. "For God's sake, Chance, I'm no longer your kitten. I'm not sure I ever was."

"You were. Are. But I'll play your game. The letter...Avery."

"Game? You seriously think I'm playing some kind of game?" She shakes her head. "Get out."

I stand my ground. "You're right. I shouldn't have used that word. But I'm not going anywhere. Not until you tell me about this supposed letter."

Her eyes turn to fire. "*Supposed* letter? You're something else."

"I want to know about it."

She looks up at the ceiling, crosses her arms over her

chest. While the action covers her perfect tits, it slides the hem of her shirt up a few inches.

"You *wrote* it," she snaps.

I never wrote a letter, but as I look at Avery, I see no evidence of deceit in her countenance. Still, I could be misreading her. It's been a long time.

I draw in a breath. "You obviously don't like what it said."

"Get out, Chance." Her voice is soft.

And with that, I know. I know I'm not misreading her. There's a letter involved, and she thinks *I* wrote it.

And whatever was in this mystery letter is bad. Fuck.

I drop to the crappy wooden chair in the corner. I'm not going anywhere. "Show me the letter."

"I can't."

Maybe I didn't misread her after all. I lift my eyebrows. "Oh?"

"I burned it," she says. "Burned it to fucking ashes, Chance."

I ache to go to her, to touch her. I was right. I didn't misread her.

"Then tell me what it said," I say softly.

"If I tell you, will you leave me alone?"

I don't answer, only lean forward, set my elbows on my thighs. I'm not eager to hear what it said because I know it's bad. It's clearly what tore us apart. The only thing I know for sure is that I didn't fucking write it.

"It was fun, but it's over." She keeps her focus on the patterned carpet at her feet. "You're good and all, but I can't keep you. You have to know that. I'm a Bridger and you're just another pussy I fucked at the spring." She sighs. "That's about the gist of it."

I pop to my feet. "What the fuck?" I shout, knowing full well 'that I'm waking anyone else who may be sharing walls with Avery's room.

"I'm not repeating it," she says.

"You don't have to." I take a step toward her.

She retreats.

I take another step. "You think I wrote that shit?"

"It was signed by you. You mentioned the spring. You know, where I was just another pussy."

Rage pulses through me. Who the hell saw us? And she knew that she was my first. We talked about it. We...

Fuck. She thinks I lied to her. That—

I take another step toward her, trying to push down the anger because it's not directed at her. It's directed at whoever wrote the damned letter—and I have a pretty good idea who was behind it. "We were together for *two years*, Avery. I never took anyone there. Before or after you. You know it was the first time for both of us."

She blinks. "Yeah, well, it's fine. You made yourself clear with everything that you wrote before that."

I tear my hat off, fling it on her unmade bed, and run my hands through my hair. "I didn't write that! I didn't write you a letter. Do I seem like the guy to *write a fucking letter?*"

She flinches.

"Fuck, kitten. That's what happened? You got that letter and left?"

"I—"

"Was it in my handwriting? Did you recognize my signature?"

"I—" She shakes her head. "You didn't write letters, Chance. I didn't know your signature."

"You're right." I take another step. "I didn't write letters. I *don't* write letters."

She steps back again, leans against the wall. "What are you saying?" Her voice is barely more than a whisper.

I close the space between us, but I don't touch her. Since I'm taller, I bend at the waist so my eyes meet hers, which are now swimming with tears.

"Someone got between us, and I have a pretty fucking good idea of who."

She licks her lips, the color leached from her soft cheeks.

"Your father?" she whispers.

I nod, close my eyes so I don't punch my fist through the wall.

"But how—"

"It doesn't matter now." I don't want to take a second to think about how he did it. Or why. "What matters is that you're here."

I can't hold back from touching her any longer. I reach up, cup her cheek, and tip her face up to mine. "That you're mine again. You always were, kitten."

She shakes her head slightly and I tug at her silky hair.

"Say it," I snarl. A feral need to make her mine all over again, for her to know she belongs to me, takes over.

"It's not that simple."

"It is."

"Chance, I thought you hated me. Used me. That we —" She glances away. "That we had something special. That we would be together forever."

I groan, and then I kiss her. Her mouth is soft and supple, yet fierce and needy, on mine. As if she needs this contact and connection as much as I do. I break the kiss because I need to say something. She needs to hear it.

"We will have forever. Again."

11

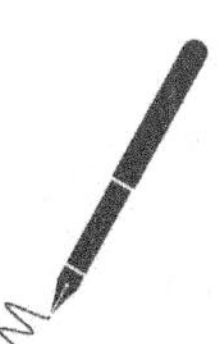

AVERY

HE DIDN'T WRITE the letter. I believe him. The man I've hated for over a decade tells me one thing and I believe him.

I'm an FBI agent, trained to read people. He was surprised. Stunned. Furious. Sweet.

If he wrote that stupid letter, why would he come to me now? I was gone all those years, and even though I've returned, he could steer clear. Avoid me. Use his brothers as intermediaries or whatever.

But he hasn't done that. I've seen him more than I've

seen Austin and Miles. Sure, part of that is because they aren't suspects.

Or because my mind always goes to Chance.

His hand is on my cheek, his blue eyes on mine. I see everything there. All the feelings we had fifteen years ago.

We may have only had one night together, but I've also had fourteen years of a constant reminder. Grady. We made a child that day from our love. Despite waiting a month after I got on the pill, it still happened. After I found out, I spent weeks trying to figure out if I'd missed a pill during that month, or if I'd miscalculated something.

All I came up with was that it just happened.

Sometimes things just happen. Those years after the letter—after we left Bayfield—are a blur to me in many ways. I existed, had my baby, and then I was forced to grow up.

Grady turned out to be the biggest blessing of my life —and also a minute-by-minute reminder of Chance Bridger.

I kept Grady away because I thought Chance didn't want me. If he didn't want me, he didn't want a kid. But now?

I'm so lost. Overwhelmed.

"I... I don't know what to say." Instinctively, I lean my cheek into his palm, feel the heat and warmth of him.

"Say you believe me," he murmurs, leaning down, his nose running along my neck.

Goosebumps break out on my skin. "I... I believe you," I whisper.

He groans, as if something like anguish and frustration are being ripped from his chest.

"Why didn't you come to me?" he pushes.

I step back then. Yes, we both know what has kept us apart was done by, most likely, his father. But there is so much unanswered.

"Because of the letter! Why would I confront you about something so cruel?"

"You trusted me with your body. Why couldn't you think to push me on something like that? Something so wrong?"

"I... I—" I turn away, not able to look at him. Tears well and slip down my cheeks. "I loved you, and as you said, I trusted you with my body. Then the letter. I thought you used me, that you got to fuck me, take my virginity and then you had a laugh with your buddies in the locker room."

"I should take you over my knee for even thinking something like that."

I want to yell at him for such words, but the look of sheer anguish on his face prevents me from it.

"I was barely eighteen! It was so intense. So honest. And then the letter was also honest."

"It was a lie!" He draws in a deep breath. "Why did you go to Arizona? I mean, that's a big fucking coincidence."

"My mom..." My mind goes blank. Why *did* we go? Mom got some money, and it came from... Where *did* it come from? Such a blur, that time. I was awash in heartbreak—young and pregnant and tossed away by the man I thought would someday be my husband.

"Your mom...what?" he asks, this time gently.

"A relative." I search my mind for the memories. "A great-aunt died and my mom was the only living descendent. It was enough to start a new life somewhere else, for both of us to get an education. It was a godsend. At just the right time, too."

"Right." He rubs his forehead. "Just the right time. Doesn't that seem a little too coincidental? I dump you in a letter and your mother comes into money to get you out of the trailer park?"

I whip my hands to my hips. "It does now. But I was a kid! A teen with a nasty Dear John letter. I wasn't thinking about whether any of it made sense. I was thankful to get the hell out of this town."

He covers his eyes, rubs his temples. "You didn't say a word. I went to your house. You were gone. I had to learn that you left from your neighbor. That older woman. Mrs. Heinz."

Mrs. Heinz. I haven't thought of her in years. She used to bake the best cookies, and every week she rinsed her hair with something that made it look blue. Whatever happened to her? She probably died alone in that trailer park.

In my mind's eye I see Chance on the steps of the old trailer. Knocking. No answer, and then hearing from Mrs. Heinz that Mom and I left. I turn then.

"Why didn't you come get me? Why didn't you question? Wonder?"

"You 'think I didn't wonder?" He makes a fist, and his blue eyes go wild. "I've wondered every single day. And I *did* go after you. I missed two weeks of school trying to find you. But you disappeared into thin air."

He steps toward me, and I retreat until I run into the wall. He cups my face again and presses his body into me.

"It's a good thing my father's dead. If I learned about what he did while he was alive, I'd have killed him."

I swallow, nod. He would have.

"You need to find out what he was into, get to the bottom of the shit that's brought you back here. Solve it. Put the guilt on *him*. All of it. You and I both know it's where it belongs."

I nod again.

"Tell me I can kiss you. Tell me I can learn your body again. To prove to you that you've always been mine. That there are no more secrets between us."

I want to tell him yes. To all of it. Because I want him to do all that. Except there's one secret left unsaid.

Grady.

I believe Chance. I do. But I won't risk my son. Not for anything. He might prove that I've always been his, but I don't know if I'm ready for him to know he's always had a son too. For now, Grady stays a secret. Until everything's revealed. Until I know the one piece of Chance Bridger that's always been mine won't be yanked away.

"Kiss me," I say, a split second before his mouth descends on mine.

12

———

Kiss me.

I don't have to be told twice. Or once. I cup the back of her head and hold her so our lips meet. I'm gentle for a moment—one quick second where I remember the feel of her, her scent, everything about being with her.

And then I'm ravenous. I delve in and our tongues meet. I lick into her, angle her head to get as deep as possible. I move my hands over her body, immediately dropping to the hem of her sleep shirt and back up, taking it with me so I tug it over her head.

Sure, we have to stop kissing for a moment, but now she's bare.

Fuck, she's not even wearing panties.

I groan as I skim over her arms, her sides, lifting to cup her breasts, and then lower to pull her to me with a hand on her ass, the other sinking between us.

"Fuck, you're soaked."

She rolls her hips and I sink a finger into her. She was tight that first—and only—time we were together. She's just as snug now.

Her inner walls clench and I add a second finger. She goes up on her toes as I work her.

Our lips part and she pants, rolling her hips.

I watch. How can I not? She's gorgeous. As perfect as I remember, even more so. At eighteen, she hadn't grown into the womanly curves she has now. A lush roundness to her breasts, her hips.

We aren't virgins any longer, and she knows what she wants.

"Greedy pussy," I whisper in her ear as her cheeks flush and her mouth opens on a moan.

I rub my palm over her clit. I'll take her, but not before I watch her come.

When she does, her cry echoes off the walls. Only when she slumps against me do I pull my fingers free. Instead of fumbling for my dick as I would have way back when, I put my dripping fingers to my mouth and lick them clean.

Her taste... *Fuck*.

I scoop her up, carry her the few feet to the unmade bed, lower her to it, and drop to my knees at the edge. She's wilted so it's easy to move her as I want. I throw her legs over my shoulders and look at the treasure before me.

I didn't get to do this before, to taste her.

"Chance," she moans as she tangles her fingers in my hair

I'm ravenous for her, to get her essence on my tongue, to learn what makes her moan, what makes her drip for me. I'm tempted to stay here, eat her for hours...

But I don't tease her. No.

We've had almost fifteen years of it and I won't wait a second longer to give Avery pleasure.

I push her to the brink and then let her glide over. She offers a whimper and a deep clench of her inner muscles.

"Chance, please," she breathes.

I slide up her body, kissing my way over her heated skin. "What do you need? I'll give it to you."

When I'm hovering over her, she blinks her eyes open and smiles. An open, honest smile that I haven't seen in so long.

"In me. Please."

I open my belt buckle and get my jeans undone, my cock out in record time. I don't do more than push my pants out of the way before I'm over her and nudging at her entrance.

I hold her gaze as I thrust deep.

And pretty much die of the most perfect pleasure.

I groan. Growl. Moan. Whatever the sound, it's ripped from me.

"Mine," I say as her pussy flutters, adjusting to being filled. I'm not small and she sure as hell remembers now.

"Chance."

I pull back. Thrust deep again.

"Mine," I repeat.

"Yours." She rocks her hips up in time.

"Nothing's going to keep us apart now. Nothing between us."

She stills, holds my gaze.

"What?" I ask as sweat drips down my brow.

"Nothing. I…" Her eyes practically roll back in her head as I roll my hips, fucking her more deeply.

I pull out, flip her over, and lift her onto her knees.

"Head down, kitten. Good girl."

She's in position and I take her from behind. I can watch my cock disappear into her perfect pussy this way. Go deep. Make her mine.

I fuck her hard. She meets me with every thrust.

"That's it. Take what you need."

I won't last. Not this first time, so I hook an arm around her, pull her up so she's sitting on my thighs. I cup her breast with my palm and I rock into her.

"You and me. Always."

I reach down, find her swollen, sensitive clit, and circle it.

She moans. A gush of arousal coats my cock and I don't stop.

"Come and I'll follow you," I murmur in her ear.

One, two deep strokes and she falls. Lost in my arms.

I can't resist her any longer, pulling her down hard onto me and filling her. Pulsing deep and giving myself over to the best orgasm of my life.

This.

Avery.

It's everything.

Nothing will stop me from having her.

Nothing.

13

VERY

GUILT.

It's eating at me as I lie in Chance's arms. I want so badly to trust him. To allow myself to love him and let him back into my life. I'm in bed with him. That's huge, but not enough.

I can't get consumed by the chemistry between us. We've always had that. From the start, Chance and I made sparks when we were in the same room together. Even now, years and years later, it's amazing. Like nothing I ever shared with another man. I didn't know what it was. Chance is attractive, but it's not only that. He's charismatic. Rough. Gruff, too. Intense. Potent. He's also gentle. Demanding. Possessive.

He's an incredible lover. All those adjectives focused on me when clothed is one thing. But naked? When his weight is pressing me into a bed? Devastating. I'm in trouble here, because I know what it feels like with my heart on the line. I lost him once. I'm not sure if I can handle it again.

We have a lot to talk about. To work through. First, I have to solve this case. Then I'll figure out what to do, whether I can trust Chance enough to allow him into Grady's and my life.

I'm expecting the DNA results from forensics today, and if Mom came through, I should have a package waiting containing one of Grady's hairs.

All of that means I can't lie here basking in the afterglow. I have to get up and get to work.

Chance didn't let me sleep on a different side of the bed from him. No, I'm wrapped in his hold as if he's afraid I'll disappear. I ease out of Chance's arms and leave the bed, the warmth of his embrace.

"Kitten?" His voice is a soft rasp.

"Work," I say. "A lot on my plate today."

"Do you get time off for lunch?" He rolls onto his back.

I look down at him. God, why is he so sexy? His auburn hair is a mess...and his chest? Amazing. He looks like he belongs in a sexy man calendar with the sheet riding low on his hips.

I look away. If I keep staring at him, I'll end up with his dick back inside me. I'm sore in a delicious way, not used to having sex, but also not used to a dick like Chance's. Not a bad thing, but...

God, it's so complicated.

"You going to answer?"

"Sorry. Lunch? Not today. Too busy. I'll eat with Jarvis at my desk."

"Dinner then."

"I don't think—"

He pushes himself out of bed and comes up behind me. The warmth of his body permeates mine, and his cock is hard against my back. He nibbles on my earlobe and his hand reaches around and cups my breast. "Not taking no for an answer, kitten. I'll give you lunch. But dinner? You're mine."

I sigh. I don't have the strength to argue with him, even though I know I should. Except being with him is what my heart wants. What I *need.* "Dinner. Fine. But for now, I have to get ready for work."

I step away, and—

In a flash he's turned me around, pushed me against the wall, lifted me, and set me on his hard cock. Just like that. I moan at the thick feel of him deep inside me. The slight burn at his entry. But I hook my heels into his ass and hang on because I need what he's giving.

"God, you're so fucking wet," he growls.

I am. "Don't have time…"

But I'm lost already. Lost in a sea of passion and desire, as he fills me, completes me. I let my eyes flutter closed as he rocks his hips up.

"Look at me, kitten," he commands. "Don't let your eyes stray from mine. Watch my eyes as I fuck you."

I open them instantly, obeying. I don't obey anyone, but this doesn't frighten me. He's the only one who can control me. It was through my heart that I submitted to him. He always took care of me. Satisfied me. By giving in, I loved him. Now? It's as if nothing changed, as if time had stood still. I want to look at Chance. I want to look into his gorgeous blue depths, and I want to see…

Love.

True love.

True love that was never lost.

But true love that will never be the same…because *we* aren't the same. I have secrets.

I push that thought to the side and keep my gaze locked on his as he pumps, pumps, pumps, nudging my clit with each thrust.

My nipples are hard, and his chest hair is teasing them. I want his mouth there, between my legs, everywhere. Our lovemaking last night was beautiful, but we didn't touch each other enough. He didn't suck my nipples. I didn't suck his cock.

And now?

There just isn't time.

So I take what I can. Stare into those eyes. Capture the love I see there and hold it in my heart.

For in the days to come, I'll need to remember it. While he wants me, wants all of me, he doesn't know everything. When he learns the truth, will he want me? Will he want Grady?

That question is why I don't tell him. Because I can' risk my own heart, but I won't risk Grady.

Still, *this* is fucking, pure and rough. I'll take what I can. Give it in return. I need it. He's as lost in me as I am in him. He's right there with me, and that has me letting go.

I shatter.

I come all over his hard cock, letting the currents flow through me and around me and go crashing into my pussy.

"Yeah, kitten," he pants out. "Just like that. Come for me." He plunges into me with one last thrust.

We share the climax, come together, and in that precious moment, I let myself believe that everything will work out fine.

But only for that moment.

Our gazes are still locked, and Chance eases me from the wall, and I slide off his cock.

"You're so beautiful." He reaches out and brushes my hair back, as if he can't stop touching me.

"And you're magnificent."

Do his cheeks flush a little at my words? Maybe, or maybe he's already flushed from our morning workout. Either way, he looks amazing, and I'm more in love with him than ever.

Who am I kidding? I've always loved him. How could I not? He gave me Grady.

I swallow. "I... I *really* have to get to work."

"Yeah. I understand. I should too. I've been way too easy on Austin and Miles lately." He chuckles.

"Oh?"

"Yeah. I kick their asses regularly making them do ranch work."

"Why?"

He wrinkles his forehead as he grabs his boxers off the floor where he shucked them earlier. "What do you mean why?"

I shrug, grabbing my bra and working my arms through the straps. "You have hands for that."

He pulls the boxers up so they settle low on his hips. "I do, but I've always worked the ranch."

True. He always said his muscles came from ranch work. "I mean, why are you doing it now? You're the boss."

This time he shrugs. "I like it, Avery. It...saved me."

I raise my eyebrows as I reach behind me and fasten the clasp.

"When you left," he continues, moving on to his jeans, "I needed something. I found it—or at least something that helped, nothing could replace you—in hard work. Ass-busting work. Now I can't imagine myself not doing it."

I cock my head. The expression on his face is serene. He's not fabricating one bit. "The billionaire rancher who does grunt work," I say softly.

"Don't ever look down on grunt work."

I chuckle. "Are you kidding? I grew up at the trailer park, remember? Any work is good work. I think it's wonderful that you help around the ranch."

"I do more than help, kitten. It's my ranch. I don't *help*. I *do* everything. I feed the stock some days, build fencing on others. Clean the stables. Hell, I've even been known to shovel manure."

"That's endearing."

He laughs. "Shoveling manure? I'll be sure to tell my brothers that. Not that they need to be any more endearing to their women. They're so in love it's kind of sickening." He touches my cheek. "Though I'm feeling a little sick myself…"

No. No, no, no. This has to stop. I need to get ready for work. If he keeps talking, he may say…

And I can't hear that. Not yet. Not while I'm keeping such a big secret from him. I rush toward the bathroom, snagging my panties on the way. "I'm out of time."

Before I close the door, he stops me with his big bare foot. "Dinner. Should I pick you up here or at the sheriff's office?" He gives me two options, which means it's happening no matter what answer I choose.

"Depends on the time."

"You tell me," he says. He stands there in only his jeans, and they aren't even buttoned. God, he's so amazing I want to tug him back to bed even though we just fucked. I want more. I'm insatiable with him.

"Okay. How about seven? Pick me up here."

He nods. "Good enough. I'll get out of your hair for now." He brushes his lips over mine, so sweetly in contrast to how he took me against the wall. "Until tonight. And kitten?"

I arch a brow.

"If you wear panties later, they may not make it."

AN HOUR LATER, after picking up the package from Mom at the front desk of the motel–she came through just as I hoped–I'm sitting across from Jarvis at our table in the corner of the sheriff's office searching my inbox.

"Eureka!" I say.

"Good news?" Jarvis cocks his head.

I lean in to read. "From Dr. Hayes. It's the DNA results from underneath Joey Hopkins's fingernails. Now to run them..." I plug the results into the database and then I call Dr. Hayes.

"Hayes," he says into my ear.

"Dr. Hayes, it's Special Agent Avery Marsh. I just got your email, and I'm running the sample through the database. But I need a favor."

"What can I do for you?" he asks.

"I have a sample I need DNA analysis on. A rush."

"I can give you the name of the nearest lab, but it'll be in Billings," he says.

Not great, but expected. "Yeah, I figured as much. Can they do a quick turnaround like you did?"

"They should be able to do twenty-four to forty-eight hours," he says. "That's standard."

I frown. "I need better than standard."

Silence.

"Dr. Hayes?"

"I have to go. Someone just walked into my office. I'll give you a call right back."

"But the lab in Billings—"

The call drops.

Great. Just great. He'd better call me back pronto. Who could have walked into his office more important than an active case?

My phone rings while it's still in my hand. Hmm. Not a number I recognize. "Marsh," I say.

"Agent Marsh, it's Dr. Nolan Hayes."

I stop my jaw from dropping because I thought he had someone to tend to. "Hi. Where are you calling from?"

"I need you to call me back in five minutes."

"But—" Then it dawns on me. "Of course. Thanks."

He wants me to call from a burner. Not a problem. Jarvis and I keep several available at all times. Some of them McGuinness knows about. Others, he doesn't.

I rise. "I'll be back in a few," I tell my partner, who gives me a questioning look, but stays quiet. He knows I'll fill him in if it's case related. I head out to the rental car, unlock it, and pull out one of the burners from the safe in the trunk. Then I take a little walk across the parking lot. When I'm a safe distance away from the sheriff's office, I return Dr. Hayes's call.

"Agent Marsh?" he says into my ear.

"Yeah, it's me, Dr. Hayes."

"I'm going to text a number to this phone," he says. "It's a colleague of mine in Billings who runs a lab. He's the best in the business and he can usually get results back within a day. It's still early. If you hurry, he can probably take care of you by the end of the day."

This is a surprise. "Really? How?"

"I don't ask, but I can vouch for the accuracy of his results. The problem is that it will cost you."

In this case, when it comes to clearing Chance, it doesn't matter. I tell him so. "I don't care. I'll pay him."

"You sure? It's ten grand a pop."

I nearly drop the phone. "You're serious?"

"Yeah. But if this is official business, just run it through the bureau. But it'll take the regular twenty-four to forty-eight hours."

Official business? Getting my son's DNA to prove or disprove his biological father's guilt? I suppose it's business, but...

"That's what I'll do then. Thanks for the offer, though, Hayes."

"You sure?"

I sigh, debating whether my savings account can take such a hit. "Maybe. I don't know. Let me see if something comes up through the database first."

"This is a one-time offer, Marsh. And I don't give this guy's info out freely."

"Then why'd you offer it to me?" The sun gets in my eyes so I turn and face the other way.

"Something in your voice," he says. "What's going on?"

"You wouldn't believe me if I told you. Thanks for trusting me, though."

I end the call quickly, replace the burner in the car, and hightail it back into the office.

Just in time to see something pop up from the database.

14

HANCE

THE FABULOUS FOURSOME—SADIE'S name for them, not mine—are all seated at the breakfast table when I return to the house.

"Nice of you to grace us with your presence." Austin smirks at me.

"Looks like you finally took my advice," Miles drawls, looking me over as if he can tell by looking at me that I spent the early morning with Avery. That we fucked not once, but twice.

"You okay, Chance?" Carly asks with a touch of innocence. She's beautiful and kind, but too fragile for me. I instantly compare her to Avery. There is no comparison. "You look a little flushed."

Miles lets out a guffaw. "He's just fine."

Then Carly reddens, catching on. "Oh. So you and Avery worked things out, then?"

Austin smiles and hides it behind his coffee mug.

"Looks like Miles and I weren't the only ones with a conflict of interest in this case," Sadie offers, with a smile of her own.

The four of them all look so pleased with themselves that I want to puke. Except I can't get this stupid fucking smile off my own face. I head to the counter and pour myself a cup of joe. I don't kiss and tell, no matter whether they know what I've been up to or not.

"What would you like for breakfast?" Louisa asks me, turning away from the sink and wiping her hands on a dish towel.

"Whatever the peanut gallery is having is fine." I head to the table to join my brothers and their women.

They're all noshing on what looks like French toast. I'm not much into sweets at breakfast—I like my protein—but one inhale of the buttery cinnamon goodness has me singing a different tune. When Louisa slides a plate in front of me, I grab my fork and dive in.

"Thanks," I tell her.

"You going to clue us all in?" Austin asks.

I shove the forkful of toast into my mouth, effectively ending any chance of a reply. The eggs, butter, and maple syrup make it rich and delicious. I chew and swallow, and then find four sets of eyes all staring at me.

"What?" I ask innocently.

"Come on," Sadie says. "You watched the rest of us fall down the rabbit hole. We want to see you happy, Chance."

"He looks pretty happy from where I'm sitting, babe," Miles says with a chuckle.

I glare at my brother. "I think the port-a-potties on the west quadrant need cleaning today, and you look like just the man for the job."

He laughs. "Oh hell, no. I shoveled manure when you asked but I draw the line at human shit."

In reality, the port-a-potties have to be cleaned by a company that specializes in hazardous waste, but I couldn't help giving him shit. Damn, I'm in way too good of a mood.

By the looks on their faces, it surprises them. Was I really a grump? Yes. Did Avery seem to pull me out of it? Hell, yes. Was it the sex or her? Both. Because sex with Avery was the best I ever had.

"I've gone way too easy on you two the last couple days," I say, still chuckling. "That's over."

"I'm with Miles," Austin wipes his mouth with his

napkin. "No way in hell am I going near those portable johns."

"Fine." I shove another bite of breakfast into my mouth, chew, swallow. "I'm sure I can find something else for us today."

"Make it something that doesn't involve feces of any kind," Austin says. "Otherwise, my bro here and I are out."

I can't help it. I smile. Then I laugh. I'm happy, damn it. I'm fucking happy.

Avery and I are together.

Avery and I will always be together. We just need to get this case out of the way so nothing stands between us and her sitting beside us at the breakfast table.

"Tell us a little," Carly prompts. "I've never seen you with that look on your face."

She hasn't worked at the ranch for long, so her depth of experience on this topic is pretty shallow. The same goes for all of them. Only Louisa knows how grumpy I've been. For years.

I sigh and take a drink of hot coffee. "Nothing to tell."

"You're full of it, bro." Austin rises. "I'm going into town with Carly to pick up a package at the post office."

"Antibiotics," Carly adds. "For one of the pups. We're running low so Lexie ordered some more and she asked me to get them this morning."

"Good enough," I tell her and then turn to Austin.

"But why do *you* need to go? There's work to be done around here."

"I want to accompany my lady into town." Austin takes Carly's hands and pulls her out of her chair. "We'll be back in an hour."

I roll my eyes because 'he knows she can make it to town and back on her own just fine. Still, he wants to be with her. I can't say I blame him. "Fine. But if you're set on getting that billion, you need to do your share around here."

"Got it, General"—he salutes—"but have you forgotten that today is the day I'm making arrangements for my mom's rehab in Billings?"

"Shit." That's right. Austin's mom, after much argument, is moving here. With her recent accident and her MS, she needs to be near family. She and Austin decided that it was best with her closer. In Billings, Austin can visit. When she's released, she can come here. Their business is in Seattle, but her health comes first. "Sorry. So you get the day off, I guess." I look to Miles, and a strange feeling of benevolence comes over me. "You know what? You take the day off too."

Miles's jaw drops and he looks to the ceiling. "Just checking to see if any pigs are flying overhead."

Sadie gives him a playful swat.

"Hey, a mere minute ago he wanted us swabbing

latrines, and now I get the day off? It's got to be some kind of miracle. Or magical pussy." Miles rises and motions to Sadie. "Let's go before he changes his mind."

"He won't change his mind." Sadie smiles. "He's in love."

They leave, and I finish my breakfast in peace.

With that same damned smile on my face.

———

AFTER A SHOWER, I text my foreman to find out where he needs extra help today. While it's my ranch and I'm in charge, he runs the place. I couldn't do it without him. Before he responds, my phone rings.

It's Shankle. These days, I'm not sure if he's going to share good or bad news.

"Chance Bridger," I say into the phone.

"Hey, Chance. Tom Shankle. You got a minute?"

"Only about a minute." I don't want him fucking with my mood. "What's up?"

"I need a file from your father's office."

"Then come on over and get it. You know I don't go in there."

Not the old man's office. That was where he doled out whatever punishment he thought I deserved for whatever stupid shit he decided I'd done. Never mind that he was wrong most of the time. I need to clean that space out, exorcise it so it's just a room. The house is mine now. Mine and my brothers'. Jonathan Bridger's dead.

"I know, but I need your help. If you won't go in, get one of your brothers."

I inhale slowly. I'm being ridiculous. I'm a grown man, and I can go into that stupid office.

"Never mind." I rise to my feet and carry my plate to the sink. Louisa's there and I hand it off with a whispered thanks. "I have to face the place sooner or later. What do you need?"

"Jonathan kept hard copies of all documents concerning his outside businesses in the large oak file cabinet."

I make my way through the hallways of the large ranch house to my father's den. The door is shut, but it's unlocked. I turn the knob. "I'm pretty sure he keeps that file cabinet locked."

When I was young, I saw him lock that sucker up. I'm not sure if it was to keep me out or to keep the papers in.

"Not anymore," Shankle counters. "I keep it unlocked now so I can get what I need. I'm looking for some missing documents concerning Racehorse Hauling."

I raise my eyebrows as I slowly enter the office. "What kind of missing documents?"

Shankle coughs and then clears his throat. "Excuse

me. My partner in the white-collar crime division of our firm is working with the EPA and the DOJ, and some key documents seem to be missing from some of your father's filings. We can't find them online."

I roll my eyes. "Shocking."

Another throat clear. "Get into the cabinet and look for anything marked Racehorse Hauling."

I have no idea why he didn't empty the files and take them to his office.

"You think my father would be stupid enough to mark something Racehorse Hauling when he was using them to transport and illegally dispose of hazardous waste?"

"For God's sake." Shankle coughs again. "You're probably right. You won't know what you're looking for. I'll come do it myself."

"You could have saved yourself ten minutes if you'd done that," I say. "When should I tell Louisa to expect you?" I'll be out on the range and like usual, not around to deal with house things. Like answering the front door.

"Sometime after noon," he says. "Brazee is going to be pissed. He wants this stuff yesterday."

"Then the two of you should have come over yesterday. Goodbye."

After ending the call, I turn to leave the dreaded space when my phone, still in my hand, vibrates with a text.

My heart jumps. Maybe it's Avery. But disappointment

looms. It's spam. I delete it quickly and then, instead of leaving as I planned, I take a look—a real look—at the room that was Jonathan Bridger's lair.

And lair—a fierce or dangerous animal's hideout—is definitely the right word. I always knew the bastard was evil, but I didn't know *how* evil. How *criminal*.

"What secrets do you hold?" I ask out loud to the quiet room. With the door closed, the room is musty, but it's as neat as a pin. Louisa's doing.

For an instant, I actually expect the space—or my father's ghost—to answer.

No answer comes, of course, and I stand tall. Inhale.

It's just a room. Just a fucking room.

Getting Avery back has given me something.

Not courage, exactly, because I was never *afraid* to come in here. No, fear has never been my problem. I stopped being afraid of my father at age thirteen, when I grew taller than he was. By sixteen, my muscles were bigger than his. Many times I imagined pummeling him into a pulp, but one thing stopped me.

Avery. My love for Avery. She deserved better than an adolescent who used his fists to mete out justice. Even on an asshole parent who deserved it.

Nor did I stay away because of bad memories. I have the memories anyway—the image of my father sitting behind the grand oak desk, telling me what a disappointment I was, how much of a whore my mother was, how *I* was the reason she left.

But that's still not why I steer clear of the office.

The reason is actually simple.

The room represents my father, represents everything I *never* want to be. Staying away became a habit after a while.

But today, something is different. I'm whole again. So much time passed that I forgot what being whole felt like. Avery took a piece of my heart when she disappeared, and now it's back in place.

And this is just a room.

Simply a room.

Jonathan's dead and buried. He's not coming back.

Floor to ceiling bookshelves line the wall opposite the desk, divided by a gas fireplace. I'm not sure my father ever read a book, but he surrounded himself with them anyway. All the classics, leatherbound, on the right side of the fireplace. On the left are business books and journals, including agriculture and ranching references.

I take a closer look. This all belongs to me now—well, to my brothers and me—and maybe I can learn something. I peruse the titles until I come to one that makes me laugh out loud.

Journal of Business Ethics.

Ethics. Right. I'm supposed to believe my father ever cared about anything that's in this journal.

I slide my fingers over the spine. Then, curiosity tugs at me and I pull the book off the shelf—

"What the f—"

Something clicks, and the bookshelf moves toward me, like a door.

I gape at the revealed space, my jaw dropped.

My father has a fucking secret room.

15

 VERY

"YOU GET A MATCH?" Jarvis asks.

I scan the computer screen, tapping on keys. "Just a minute. I need to get to the right place."

I continue to move through screens until—

"Damn." I smile, an invisible weight lifting from my shoulders. "I got something."

"Jonathan or Chance?" For all of our investigating, it's been one or the other. That's what's been swirling in my head. While I trust Chance, I still have–had–a nagging doubt because of the letter. He didn't write it, but I've had fifteen years of thinking he did.

"Neither." I send a silent thanks upward that I didn't take that name from Hayes. I don't need to bother with Grady's hair sample now. And Chance is in the clear. Thank God!

"It's some person named Eugene Markus Chubb," I continue. "His DNA is on file for"—I scan through the information as quickly as I can—"looks like he was a suspect in an armed robbery outside of Helena about ten years ago, but his DNA cleared him." I shake my head. "Too damned bad for him that it's still on file because it's a fucking match, Jarvis. A fucking match!"

"Chubb." Jarvis narrows his eyes at me, tapping his finger on the table. "That sounds vaguely familiar to me."

"Yeah, to me too." I pull up the files on the case and do a search for the name. "Here it is. Someone by the name of Gene Chubb answered a phone when Miles Bridger dialed a number he found in a journal that presumably belonged to Joey Hopkins. I'll be damned. I think we found our killer."

My heart dances. I don't need to use the hair Mom got from Grady. It's not Chance! Not that I thought it was. Not really. But I'm elated that I can clear him now. That my trust in him wasn't wrong.

I didn't doubt him. I doubted me.

"You got an address for Chubb?" Jarvis asks.

I scan the screen. "Shit. No physical address is listed.

But there's a PO Box in Billings."

"He was a suspect in an armed robbery and there's no physical address listed?"

I shrug. "I guess no one cared enough to get one after he was cleared. But we'll find him, Jarvis. And then we can put this baby to bed."

"Yeehaw!" Jarvis hoots at me.

I roll my eyes. "Did you just say *yeehaw*? Didn't you learn anything from the cowboy hat nonsense?"

But I can't help but smile at his enthusiasm. It's infectious, although there's no way I'm making that sound.

"I'm going to do a quick search through government files." Jarvis taps on his computer. "I found an address for Eugene M. Chubb in Billings." He stands, grabs his keys off the table. "Let's go get him and bring him in."

THE ADDRESS JARVIS found for Gene Chubb turns out to be a prefabricated home standing alone on a plot of a couple acres. Weeds have overtaken what there is of a lawn, and a few stray cats roam around outside the house. The wind's blowing and I expect out here it never stops. I can only imagine how it is in the winter. Depressing as hell.

Jarvis parks the car on the dirt driveway, and we head to the doorway. A tattered doormat that says *Beware of Dog* sits on the spalling concrete stoop.

No doorbell, so I knock on the door, expecting to hear a dog bark.

No dog.

"Mr. Chubb?" I knock again.

No response. Not that I expected one.

"Chubb," Jarvis yells. "Open up!"

Again, no response.

I knock one last time, this time pounding my fist on the wooden door as hard as I can. "FBI, Mr. Chubb. Open up, or we're coming in!"

We have no warrant, but we have probable cause to believe a felon is inside. I nod to Jarvis, and we both draw our weapons.

I try the doorknob, and to my surprise, it turns. I open the door slowly, taking stock of the situation. "Mr. Chubb?" I call.

With Jarvis at my back, I enter. Once we're both inside, we stay back-to-back as we creep through the small home. It's in pretty good shape, decent beige carpeting and basic furniture that could have come straight out of the IKEA catalog. I inhale. Cigarette smoke hangs in the air. Someone is here or was here recently.

"Come on out, Chubb," Jarvis calls.

We walk through the living area to the kitchen. A few dishes sit in the stainless steel sink. Nothing of note, until I shift my gaze to the sliding glass door to the back. The blinds are drawn, and I open them.

On the concrete deck sits a balding man smoking a cigarette. I slide the door open, my gun drawn.

"Mr. Chubb?"

The man raises his head and then gasps when he sees my weapon. "What the fuck?"

"Special Agent Marsh, FBI. Get those hands up. You're under arrest for the murder of Joseph Hopkins."

———

"I want a lawyer," Chubb says for the umpteenth time. It's all he's said to us since we picked him up.

Jarvis and I are at the FBI office in Billings, sitting across from Eugene Chubb in one of the questioning rooms. The scent of cigarette smoke clings to the man.

"Someone from the Federal Public Defender's Office is on the way," I say, "but we've got you dead to rights on murder. Your DNA was found under the victim's fingernails. There's not much a lawyer can do for you now. You're going down."

"I'm not confessing," he replies. "I'm waiting for my lawyer, but I can tell you I don't even know the guy."

"Then don't confess," Jarvis says. "We already know you did it. Your DNA under the guy's fingernails at death? A grand jury will see it the same way. Your best bet is to talk to us."

He says nothing.

I draw in a breath. Time to bring out the big gun. "You may find it interesting, Mr. Chubb, that although it's used rarely, we *can* ask for the federal death penalty in this case."

Chubb's sunken eyes go wide.

"Agent Marsh is right." Jarvis looks down at his laptop screen. "Murder of a state or local law enforcement officer—"

"Joey Hopkins was no cop," Chubb grits out.

I raise my eyebrows. "So you *did* know him."

Chubb pins his lips shut. Yeah, he's stepped in it.

"You should have let Agent Jarvis finish," I say. "The federal government can seek the death penalty in the murder of a state or local law enforcement official or other person aiding in a federal investigation."

Though we've yet to determine whether Joseph Hopkins was aiding in an investigation, my gut tells me he was ready to turn evidence. It won't hurt to let Chubb think he could face capital punishment—even though it's unlikely.

A guard knocks and then opens the door. "Public defender's here," he says.

A young woman dressed in black pants and a white shirt enters carrying a laptop. "I'm Joycelyn Akers."

Jarvis stands and holds out his hand. "Special Agent Roy Jarvis. This is Special Agent Avery Marsh, and this is your client, Eugene Chubb."

Akers takes a seat next to Chubb. "If you two will excuse us for a moment, I'd like to confer with my client in private."

"Of course." I rise and gather my things.

Jarvis grabs his laptop and we leave the room.

"What do you think?" Jarvis asks as we walk down the hallway.

"He knows a lot more than he's letting on, for sure," I say. "I want to know why that body ended up on Bridger land. From what I know about Jonathan Bridger, he's not stupid enough to have someone killed and then tossed on his own property."

To the contrary. Jonathan Bridger was shrewdly intelligent. And evil. I knew that personally. He fucked up my life plenty. If he were alive, I'd—

I don't know *what* I'd do, but keeping me from Chance was brutal.

Jarvis nods. "I agree. There's something we're missing here."

"We can check in with the EPA investigators, see what they've found. If that whistleblower is still talking."

Jarvis sighs. "Didn't you hear?"

I frown and slow. "Hear what?"

He stops beside me, faces me. "A memo came in earlier. The poor guy was found early this morning, toes up in his bathtub."

Dead?

Early this morning. When I was in my motel room with Chance.

"Then Chubb had better talk," I say, "because our links to Bridger and Racehorse Hauling are rapidly disappearing."

We head to an open work area to wait. Jarvis leaves to get us a couple bottles of water and returns. I open mine and take a long sip, letting the liquid cool my parched throat. What a fucking day.

When my water is nearly drained, Ms. Akers approaches. "Mr. Chubb is ready to talk," she says.

I glance to Jarvis. "This should be interesting," I murmur.

Returning to the interrogation room, we take our places across from Chubb and the attorney to hear what he has to say.

16

CHANCE

Unreal.

Fucking unreal.

The *Journal of Business Ethics* is hooked by a simple string to a gate latch on the other side. So simple...and I never knew it was here.

How could I? I never come in here.

The small room is dark except for the light trailing in from my father's office. I scan the wall, find a light switch, and a fluorescent bulb bathes the room in harsh white light.

Boxes. Mountains of cardboard boxes.

God damn.

If my father was hiding anything, it's in this windowless room.

But where to begin?

The space itself isn't large—maybe twelve by twelve feet—but the boxes are piled floor to ceiling and about four rows deep.

Does Shankle know about this place? I doubt it. Shankle was my father's personal attorney for the ranching side of his business, and he swears everything was run by the book. I don't have any reason to believe otherwise, as I've had a hand in that business for the last fifteen years. I've worked the ranch. I've seen the books.

No. I won't find anything about the ranch in here.

If Shankle's shady, he wouldn't have kept these boxes here to be found. Sure, I lived in the house my entire life and never knew it existed, but hiding the evidence to crimes here? With my father dead, Shankle would be the one to go to jail if he'd helped.

I gave Miles and Austin both the day off, and that must have been divine providence because I need to be alone for this. Everything here happened before them. Before our father died. I need to work through it all on my own, get my head around everything because I was here, living, working while whatever shit he did occurred right under my nose.

He wasn't just an asshole and a shitty father, he was a criminal. Who would keep a hidden room if he didn't have shady shit to hide?

I pull the nearest box down from a stack I can reach and lift the lid. Stacked manila folders with no notation as to their contents. No notation on the box either, until I look closely. Written by hand in small letters that are hidden by the lid when the box is closed is the name *Diana Lovering*.

I drop my mouth open. Diana Lovering is Austin's mother. I pull out a folder and open it. Papers fall to the floor, and I sit down on the hardwood, gathering them. They're Diana's medical records, all about her MS. He was keeping tabs on his ex. Recently, too.

Why? I don't know, but if there's a box for Austin's mother...

There may be a box containing information on my mother.

I work like a fiend pulling down boxes, lifting the lids, and checking the contents. Most names I don't recognize. I don't find Miles's mother. I don't find my mother, Lisabeth Davies. I don't find Racehorse Hauling or Joseph Hopkins. At least not yet.

Still I keep at it, until—

"Fuck." I thread my fingers through my hair.

The name on the box I'm holding is *Linda Marsh*.

Avery's mother.

17

VERY

"FIRST OF ALL"—AKERS clears her throat—"I could report the two of you for threatening my client with the death penalty."

"It *could* apply here," Jarvis says, not the least bit intimidated.

"Yes, and I *could* sprout a beanstalk out of my ass." Akers stares him down.

I force myself not to smile. Too bad we're on opposite sides. Otherwise, I think I could be friends with this woman.

"Nevertheless," she continues, "based on the evidence

in this case, I've advised my client to cooperate with the two of you."

"So he's confessing?" I drop into the chair across from them.

"Go ahead, Mr. Chubb." Akers nods to the guy.

Chubb rubs his hands over his cheeks and I'm not sure if he's nervous or needs another hit of nicotine. "Truthfully? I'm tired of hiding. I'm tired of the whole fucking thing."

"You don't need to volunteer information," Akers says. "Just tell them what we talked about."

He nods. "Right. Joey Hopkins wasn't working on a federal investigation. At least not to my knowledge. But he *was* collecting information."

"On Racehorse Hauling?" Jarvis asks.

Another nod. "Yeah. He worked there. His old man recommended him to me."

"You know Curt Hopkins?" I ask, trying to put all the players together.

Chubb nods. "He and I worked together on a few construction projects back in the day. Anyway, one day on a job I wasn't wearing my hard hat, and Curt pushed me out of the way when a steel beam fell. He took a huge whack on the head. Even with the hard hat, he was never the same after that. His skills suffered, and he started drinking. But the fucker—"

"Mr. Chubb," Akers admonishes.

I hold back laughter. She's telling him not to use the F-word after she talked about something sprouting out of her ass. Still like her, though.

"Whatever. Sorry." He rolls his eyes. "Anyway, he saved my life that day. The beam would have taken me out for sure. I think he did it so he wouldn't be shut down though. I mean, a workman's comp claim like mine, where I wasn't wearing a hard hat when I was supposed to... you know what I mean. But still." He pauses a moment, coughs into his hand. "So when I heard of this opportunity with Racehorse Hauling, I brought him in. I knew his business was suffering, and it was suffering because of me. If he'd let me croak that day he'd still have his faculties and he wouldn't have started drinking."

I'm not so sure about that, but it definitely could have been the start.

"Is any of this in our records?" I ask Jarvis.

He looks my way. "Not that I've seen, but we weren't looking at Curt Hopkins as a suspect."

He's already in jail for attempted murder of 'his own daughter, who's also a police detective.

"True, and Sadie's been estranged from her father, so she wouldn't know. Go on, Mr. Chubb. What was the opportunity you found with Racehorse Hauling?"

"I swear to God I thought it was on the up and up at first. My criminal days were behind me."

"Your criminal days?" I ask. "All we have in your record is that you were a suspect in an armed robbery, but you were cleared."

"Go ahead," Akers says to Chubb.

"I was good," he says with a smirk. "I never got caught."

"Doing what?" Jarvis demands.

"Does it matter?" Akers asks. "Whatever he did isn't the least bit relevant to your investigation."

Jarvis sighs. "Not at this point, I guess. Go on."

"I got a shit ton of money for hauling freight into Canada," he says. "And when I say a shit ton, I mean a shit ton. I didn't know what the hell I was hauling and I didn't care. I took their money, and I sent half of it to Curt."

"Why?" Jarvis asks.

I want to know as well.

"Because the fucker—" He looks at Akers. "Sorry. The *man* saved my life. He was a mess. So I did what I could to help him. When he sent his son to me for a job, I hired him too. Things went fine for a couple years. I kept Joey on routes night and day so no one knew where he was."

"So he didn't disappear?" I ask.

"Depends on the definition of disappear, I guess."

Chubb snorts. "He did take a little time off to donate a portion of his liver to some friend of his."

"So that's what happened," I say. "Which friend?"

"I don't know, but they were a match, apparently. Anyway, Joey was a good guy, but not the brightest. He did what he was told. But when he came back to work after the liver donation, he was...different. Said he'd had an epiphany in the hospital or something and he wasn't comfortable with what was going on. He started asking questions I couldn't answer."

"Couldn't answer?" Jarvis asks.

"Damned right. I didn't have the answers because I never asked the questions. Don't look a gift horse in the mouth and all."

"Right," I say, "and you, an admitted former criminal, didn't stop to think you could be breaking the law. Not once in all that time."

He drums his fingers on the table. "Money kind of puts stars in your eyes. Besides, no one was getting hurt."

I shake my head. "For God's sake. Just get to the part where you killed Hopkins. You know, where someone *got hurt*."

He flushes. "I didn't want to. I mean, his father saved my life. But someone was blackmailing me."

"Jonathan Bridger," I say. It's not much of a stretch.

He nods once again. "Yeah, but I didn't know it at the time."

"How did you find out?" Jarvis asks.

"Joey. He told me it was Bridger. Those were his last words after we fought, after I managed to inject him with the fentanyl that was left for me to use on the guy."

I've been with the FBI for years, and it still surprises me how murderers talk so nonchalantly about taking a human life. "So then what?" I prod.

"I took the body, went onto Bridger land, and tossed it into a creek. I figured if I was going down, so was Bridger. I had nothing to lose at that point."

Again, he says it so casually, as if killing a guy and then transporting and dumping the body with the intent to frame someone else is no big deal. Shows premeditation. I hope he gets enough money for black market cigarettes in prison.

"How did Joey know Bridger was behind it?" I ask. We might have Joey's killer, but we need this guy to give up Jonathan Bridger.

He shrugs. "I don't know, and I didn't ask, since I was in the middle of taking his life, lady."

"My client is pleading guilty," Akers says. "He'll sign an affidavit under penalty of perjury attesting to the claims he made today. Then I expect the two of you to maybe go a little easy on him with sentencing."

"A little easy? Uh...he killed a man," I say to her. "Premeditated."

"He did. But he has cooperated and you're getting information you wouldn't otherwise have regarding your case."

"Our case is closed," Jarvis says. "And the DOJ will decide on what to recommend for sentencing."

Chubb sighs. "You know? I've got to say I almost feel a relief. I'm glad I'm done hiding."

"Another one for the archives," I say to Jarvis, closing my laptop. The two of us are done. Jonathan Bridger's dead. The DOJ can deal with Chubb. "I have somewhere to be."

I hop to my feet. Time to see Chance.

I want to be the one to tell him he's cleared. That the case is over.

18

CHANCE

I'M ABOUT to open the box marked with Avery's mother's name when I hear Louisa calling my name. I rise quickly, replacing the bookshelf. Louisa won't look for me in here. She knows I never set foot in this office and she only comes in to dust' periodically. Still...I don't want anyone to know about the secret room. At least not yet.

Her voice dims as she walks farther from the office. Good. Gives me a chance to get out. I close the hinged section of bookshelf behind me, then leave the room. I walk briskly through the house.

"Louisa?" I call, heading her way. "Here I am. What do you need?"

She turns and puts a hand to her chest. A smile is on her kind face. "Goodness. Where have you been?" She looks around as if I magically appeared. I'm a big guy and can't sneak anywhere—except out of a secret room I didn't know was in my own house.

"Just doing some work," I reply. It's not a lie, exactly.

"Special Agent Marsh is here. She's waiting for you in the living room."

I lift my eyebrows, my heart kicks up, and my dick swells. Avery is here? I whisk past Louisa without another word, although I can't miss the even bigger smile on her face. She's worked here since I was a kid and knows all about Jonathan Bridger. And me. And my past with Avery. Unlike my brothers, she keeps her opinions about us being back together to herself. Smart woman.

When I reach the living room, Avery runs to me. Kisses me.

I'm too stunned to do more than wrap my arms around her and kiss her right back. Her mouth on mine, her lithe body in my arms is all I could imagine.

I've dreamed of Avery living in this house with me. Kids. Everything. I know she's skittish, even after our night together, but this? Fuck. It's better than I could have expected.

"I thought we were having dinner." I pull back just enough to meet her eyes. "Couldn't wait to see me?" I can't help the grin on my face. If Miles or Austin saw me, they'd think I'm having a stroke. I never smile...until now.

"We are. But I have news. Gene Chubb confessed to killing Joey Hopkins. The case is closed."

I blink. Chubb... Chubb. The name sounds familiar. "The guy Miles called?"

She nods. "DNA match. His DNA was in the system from an armed robbery some time ago. It matched what we found under the victim's fingernails. We picked him up and he confessed. He's a killer, but he seems to have a little bit of a conscience. Enough to be tired of holding that secret."

She's kissing along my neck as she explains. I'm not sure what's gotten into her, why she's running hot, but again, I don't ask. I love the feel of her, the way she's come to me to satisfy her needs.

"What about my father?" I angle my head so she can kiss me better.

"He wasn't involved in the murder. What he *was* involved in will be decided by the DOJ."

I think of the secret room. Of the files.

Then I stop thinking when Avery says—

"Take me to your room."

Those words coming all breathy-like from her mouth

make my dick hard and my mind blank. The news I have to share won't change in the next two or three hours, which gives me time to fuck her until we're both completely satisfied.

Everything can wait until I've taken care of Avery.

"You need to come?" I cup her ass and lift her up.

She wraps her legs around me and I carry her through the house to my room.

"God, yes. Make me come, Chance."

My dick is already leaking pre-come from the need to get in this woman. I kick the door shut behind us, then carry her to the bed, set her on her feet right at the foot of it.

Her hands are on my shirt and she tugs, the snaps popping one by one.

"I love these shirts." She roams her hands over my chest.

I hold her wrists, saying nothing.

She looks up at me. "What?"

"I'm all for you wanting to get it on, but what's changed, Avery?"

She shrugs a slim shoulder. "The case is over. You're innocent."

"You didn't think I was?" I ask. I don't release her wrists. I need to know how she feels. If she thought I was guilty. "Did you think I was a murderer?"

Her eyes widen. "No. God no. But that letter, Chance. It was so...mean. Absolutely cruel and callous."

"Callous enough to make you think I could take a life?"

She shakes her head vehemently. "No. Not really. I just... I had doubts."

I imagine that's true. I doubted her just as long.

"The case was in the way," she say. "I'm...relieved it's over."

"Nothing between us now, is there, kitten?" I set her hands on my shoulders so I can kiss her.

I don't know how long we stand there, making out like high schoolers, but we finally tear our lips apart.

"Nothing between us," I repeat.

Her eyes meet mine. They're blurry with need, but there's something there. Uncertainty? Doubt? I blink and it's gone.

She drops to her knees.

"Oh fuck," I murmur.

She works on my belt buckle, then opens my jeans. I help her push the denim down my hips along with my boxers until my dick springs free.

She grasps the base and licks it like a fucking lollipop.

"Jesus, Avery."

She never did this when we were kids. The sight of her

on her knees before me, gripping my dick and taking it into her—

"Fuck..." I growl.

I grab her hair and tug. Her eyes lift to meet mine as she continues to suck and lick, taking me as deep as she can, then stroking me in tandem with her tight fist.

I'm not going to last. The need I have for her is too great. The vision she makes before me. Everything.

I pull back and her mouth comes off me with a pop. I pick her up and toss her on the bed. She bounces and I hook her ankle, tugging off one shoe, then the other.

Then I get her pants off, snagging her panties with them.

Another grip on her ankle and I pull her to the edge of the bed, her ass barely hanging off.

"Feet on the edge. Good girl. Spread nice and wide. Just like that."

The sight of her, half dressed, legs spread, pussy dripping and ready for me.

My dick is dripping and my balls are aching to get in her.

Not yet. She'll come on my mouth first.

It's my turn to drop to my knees and worship her.

"Chance!" she cries the first time I lick up her slit.

Her taste bursts on my tongue and I hold her nice and wide so I can feast.

"You solved your case, sugar. Good girls get rewarded."

I don't say more. The only sounds in the room as I eat her out is her ragged breathing and my name as she moans.

She comes quickly when I sink two fingers into her wet heat and find her g-spot. She writhes and moans and I can't take another second to get inside her.

I pop to my feet, put my hands on her thighs and push them wide, then sink in.

One hard thrust and I'm home.

"Chance!"

Her pussy clenches around me and I know I won't last. I fuck her hard. Deep. Fast. Until her walls flutter around me. Until my balls draw up. Until we're both hoarse with satisfaction.

I reach between us and rub her clit, pushing her over the edge. I follow, filling her with my come. Marking her as mine in a way I've never done before.

I pull out, watch my seed slip from her as I flip her onto her stomach. She's half off the bed and I give her ass a gentle spank.

"We're not done, sugar. Just getting started."

My dick's slick with our combined fluids and I'm still hard. I fill her again, this time my passage so slick from coming inside her.

"Chance," she moans, gripping the bedding.

"That's right, say my name. You're mine, Avery. Nothing will take you from me again."

I prove that to her for hours. Giving her orgasm after orgasm until she's asleep in my bed.

Where she belongs. Sated. Sweaty and filled with my seed.

Avery Marsh is fucking mine.

19

VERY

I AWAKE, awash in a cold sweat.

For a moment, I don't know where I am, until I hear a soft snore next to me.

Chance. I'm in Chance's bed.

Chance, whose name has been cleared.

Chance, who I never stopped loving after all these years.

Chance...

Who has a son.

A freaking son.

How can I tell him about Grady? How can I *not* tell him about Grady?

I know why I awoke in a cold sweat. Only one thing makes me wake up so abruptly, brushing my arms against the chill.

I was dreaming about Grady's birth. It was hell. Pure hell, and I nearly lost my life, and I did lose my uterus. But when I was finally in the clear, and my mother placed my son in my arms...

God, it was all worth it.

It was immediate, the recognition of Chance in my son. Our son.

Now I'm with Chance. In his big bed. In the huge Bridger ranch house. I used to imagine waking up beside him. Of this house being ours. Having kids.

Until...

The letter. Mom's inheritance.

But now? I'm in Chance's bed. It seems he wants a relationship where I stay here, in his arms, in his house.

We even have a child....except Chance doesn't know the child exists.

Still, nothing is as it seems. We know each other, the youthful versions of ourselves. But there are years, well over a decade, of time where we didn't know anything about each other.

Chance is an open book. He's been here this whole

time. Working the land that looks exactly the same as when I left.

Me? I'm different. I'm not the same, naive girl I once was. I have raised a boy. Lived my life. And now? I'm the one with secrets. With the one and only thing that is a part of both of us. It should bring us together, but my stomach churns with doubt. I think Grady just might tear us apart.

Not Grady himself. Chance will adore his son. He'll want to be a part of his life.

But he'll be so angry. Angry that I kept him from his child.

Now that I'm with Chance—and I know he didn't write that letter—I don't want to let him go.

My mother told me it was best to not tell him about Grady, and I believed her. I was a scared teenager, looking to her for guidance and support. What did I know about being a mom? How could I raise a child who was so perfect and beautiful but at the same time a haunting memory of the man who didn't want me?

But we did it together. Mom and I both went to college, arranging our classes so that someone was always home with Grady.

And eventually, I moved forward. I never forgot Chance Bridger—how could I when every day I saw the miniature version of him?—but I agreed with my mother.

Grady was mine. Chance had dumped me in the cruelest way possible, and he didn't deserve to know his son. I even worried that if he knew, he might try to take him from me.

I wasn't the girl from the wrong side of the tracks any longer, but no one can compete with the Bridger money. When money talks, things happen. Like a child being given to the father.

Except...

Chance didn't write that letter.

And I've kept him from his son.

I tiptoe out of bed and head into Chance's bathroom. I inhale. It smells like him, like the outdoors with a touch of cinnamon and mint. I peek into his shower. Rosemary mint shampoo. No wonder his hair smells so good. The toilet lid is covered in forest green, and I sit down, letting my head fall into my hands.

I have no idea what time it is, but through the bathroom window I can see the translucent orange-purple of the Montana dawn. Time to get up. I have to get back to the motel, gather everything together.

Jarvis and I leave this afternoon, back to our home office in Phoenix.

The only reason we got this assignment is because the central office put out a memo asking if any field agents had any connection to Bayfield, Montana. McGuinness answered the call on my behalf. I didn't have a choice. I had to take the case.

I had to come back.

I draw in a breath.

I'm lying. I'm lying to myself, and it's got to stop. McGuiness would have let me off, especially if I'd been up front about my past with Chance. He wouldn't have wanted me involved in a case where I had a child with one of the suspects. If Chance had been the killer, my connection alone would have blown the entire prosecution.

I chose not to tell my boss the truth, just like I didn't tell Chance. I chose to come here, to dredge up my past. Did I expect to fall into bed with him again? No. Did I expect my feelings to resurface, the ones that never really went away? No.

I came anyway. I agreed to it because I wanted to see Chance Bridger, and this case gave me the perfect opportunity. I would have never come on my own, but even after all these years, I wanted to confront him about the past, ask him why he'd been so malicious.

Except he hadn't been. It was all a lie.

And I'm continuing to lie.

A soft knock on the door. "Kitten?"

I grab some toilet paper and wipe the tears from my eyes. "Yeah?"

"You okay?" he calls through the closed door.

"I'm fine. What time is it?"

"Six thirty." He chuckles. "I overslept."

"Well, you worked pretty hard last night." I open the door and melt into his arms. God, how can I walk away from this? From him? Again?

He kisses the top of my head. "Not nearly hard enough."

I look up at him, gaze into those gorgeous baby blues. "I have to go."

"You're never leaving this room." He smiles.

If only...

"I have to. Jarvis and I are going back to Phoenix. We have to file our official reports by the end of the day and then go through debriefing, which is scheduled for tomorrow morning. I already have a flight booked for eleven. I have to get to Billings."

I feel his muscles go taut. His fingers grip me a little more firmly.

"Cancel it."

Oh, how I wish. "This is my job, Chance."

"I get that. But cancel the flight, and I'll fly you back later tonight on the company's plane."

I shake my head. "I can't. I'm sorry."

He cups my cheek. "Can you at least have some breakfast?"

"I suppose." I offer a smile. "I wish things were different."

"We'll make it work this time." He thumbs the apple of my cheek. "There's no Jonathan Bridger to fuck things up. Just you and me and our life together."

"I live in Phoenix. My job is in Phoenix."

My son. My son is in Phoenix.

He offers a shrug. "So you'll get a transfer. Any field office would kill to have a superb agent like you."

"My mom's in Phoenix."

"We'll move her up here. I'll help her find a place. I'll—"

I silence him the only way I can think of in the moment. I pull his head toward me and crush our mouths together.

As our tongues tangle and entwine, I wish for a split second that the years could wash away. That we were back in that spring, making love for the first time, knowing that we'd always be together.

But fifteen years can't be erased, and though that day brought me unbearable pain, it also brought me the brightest light in my life.

Grady.

I break the kiss.

"Chance..."

He nibbles at my earlobe. "Yeah?"

"I need..."

"What? What do you need?"

I sigh. "I need you. You."

"You have me, kitten. For as long as you want me."

I turn my head, meet his lips. I believe his words. I do. But when he finds out what I've kept from him?

I push that thought to the side as he scoops me into his arms and carries me back to his bed.

In another moment, his cock is inside me and he's driving into me, beads of sweat forming at his hairline as his gaze pierces mine.

"Mine," he says, grunting. "Mine, Avery Marsh. Mine."

"Yours..." I echo.

Because I am his. I've always been his, even when I hated him. Even when I nearly died giving birth to our son. Even when I found out I'll never have another child. Even when I tried having relationships with other men and failed.

My heart, my body, my soul—it all belongs to Chance Bridger.

And I'll still belong to him when I tell him the truth.

He may leave me, but I'll still be his.

But I can't bear the thought of him leaving me.

So I'll leave.

I'll go back to Phoenix.

Back to my life.

A life without Chance Bridger.

————

AFTER JARVIS and I land in Phoenix, we go straight to the office to finish our report so we're ready for the debriefing tomorrow. Then I head to the home I share with my mother and my son. In those hours, I try not to think of Chance, of him being so far away. Of what could be if I stayed. If I did what he suggested and relocated to Montana, dragging my mother back with me.

When I walk in the door, Grady is sitting at the kitchen table, working on homework.

"Hey, sweetie," I say to him. "I'm home."

He looks up and smiles. God, it's the same smile I saw this morning on his father. The ache for Chance is familiar, and back with a vengeance. "Hey, Mom."

"No hug?"

He begrudgingly rises and walks toward me and gives me a fourteen-year old-boy hug. I know he loves me, though. When I finally let go, I look into his blue eyes, so like his father's. He's so tall and I can see how he will fill out to be big and broad.

I adopt my stern mother voice. "We need to talk about your suspension."

"Do we, Mom?" He steps back and drops into his chair,

all gangly limbs.

"Yeah. But after dinner." I give him a little bit of a reprieve. I've been gone a few days. What's a few hours more? "Where's Grandma?"

"On the service porch. Laundry."

"Okay." I lean in and kiss his fair cheek. "Get back to work. Then we're going out to dinner tonight."

"What for?"

"Because I'm home! And I solved my case. So finish up."

I head through the back way where my mom is loading the dryer with damp clothes.

"I'm home, Mom."

She widens her eyes. "Avery, I didn't expect you until later tonight."

I watch as she tosses a sock in the dryer.

"Jarvis and I finished up the report quicker than expected, so here I am. I'm taking you and Grady out to dinner."

She smiles and studies me. "You look good, honey."

"Thanks. I feel good." Then I bite my lip. I don't keep things from this woman. We've been through so much together. "Sort of. I solved the case. Chance is innocent. We found the person who killed that poor guy and threw him onto Bridger land."

"I knew you would." Mom inhales. Then again as she

looks away. "Sweetheart, you and I need to talk."

"About what?"

"About Chance Bridger."

I smile. Then I frown. Is she worried he was mean to me? That I saw him and he talked to me like he had in the letter? "I... I'm home, Mom. I'm not going back to Montana."

Those words are hard to get past my lips. I ache for Chance, but going back? I don't know how to make that work.

"He didn't write you that letter." Mom slams the dryer door shut.

"I know." I blink, process. "I— Wait. You *knew* about that?"

She won't meet my gaze. Mom takes my hand, but I yank it away from her.

"Avery..."

She knew?

She knew?

"What the hell, Mom? All these years, and you knew?" I pace the concrete floor. "You let me think that Chance could write those words? They were so mean, and that's not Chance. It's not what he would ever say to me."

"Avery." She closes the dryer door, pushes the start button, and gestures to a patio chair. "Sit down. We need to talk. Now."

20

HANCE

Pop!

Austin opens a bottle of Veuve Cliquot and pours five glasses of the sparkling wine.

"Seems like we're missing a glass," Miles says. "Where's Avery?"

"Phoenix." I run my hand over my face. I hate saying that because it's really fucking far away. I just got her back and I had to let her go again. "She had to get back to do her report, and she has a debriefing tomorrow."

"Seems like she should be here to celebrate with us,"

Austin says. "After all, she solved the case. Proved your innocence."

"I was always innocent."

"We all know that." Carly takes a glass of champagne from Austin. "None of us ever doubted you."

Sadie nods. She was on the case but stepped back when her family's involvement became clear. "Even though we were estranged, I miss my brother, and I'm glad to know he was one of the good guys. And my dad, too. If he didn't have brain damage from that accident, maybe he wouldn't have pulled a gun on me."

Miles doesn't look like he has the same generous thoughts about the man. I don't either. I can't imagine pulling a gun on my own child. At least, I figure that's how I'll feel when I actually have a child, with Avery as the mother. Curt Hopkins should never have done that. But if thinking her father wasn't all bad helps Sadie sleep better at night, I'm not going to argue.

She sighs. "I'd like to think that's the case, anyway."

"You never knew about the construction accident?" Carly asks her, wrapping her arm around Austin's waist.

"Nope." Sadie leans her head onto Miles's shoulder. "It's all news to me. I was only eight when my mom and dad divorced, and I didn't see much of my father after that. I didn't even know about his accident. And Joey…"

Miles kisses her cheek. "I'm sorry you lost your

brother. So sorry. Do you want to have a memorial service for him?"

Sadie shakes her head. "I didn't really know him. Not since I was a little girl. Sure, I have some fond memories. One time he took me sledding with the big boys. But no one around here knew him. We'll give him a proper burial, but that's it. I have my closure, Miles."

"What about your mom?" Carly asks softly. "She might like to have a service."

Sadie smiles. "She's fine. I talked to her today. We're just happy he's at peace now."

"Then I think it's time for a toast." Austin holds up his glass. "To our little brother, who, as it turns out, isn't a criminal."

I hold my glass and clink it to Austin's and can't help but smirk. "Funny."

"You know," Miles pipes in, "this has been one wild ride. Jonathan Bridger was a son of a bitch for sure, but damn, if not for him, I wouldn't have met the love of my life."

"Ditto." Austin takes a sip of his wine and looks down lovingly at Carly.

I join in, clinking my glass to everyone else's, but I can't help the thought that hovers over me. If not for my father, Austin and Miles wouldn't have met Carly and Sadie. That much is true.

But if not for my father, I never would have been separated from the love of my life.

Jonathan Bridger stole fifteen years from Avery and me, and I'm pissed off. Damned pissed off.

And the fucker's dead, so I can't even make him pay.

AFTER DINNER, when the *fabulous foursome* have excused themselves, I give Avery a call.

Hello, you've reached Special Agent Avery Marsh. I'm sorry I can't take your call right now. Please leave me a detailed message and I'll get back to you as soon as I can.

God, her voice. As if she's standing right next to me.

I'd love to leave her a detailed message—all about what I'm going to do to her as soon as we're in the same room together again...

But instead, I say, "Hi, kitten, it's Chance. You were supposed to call me when you got home safely. I want to hear your voice before I go to bed tonight, so call me. I love you."

Yeah, I said it. Just like I did all those years ago. I won't stop now.

Then I head to my father's office, let myself in, lock the door behind me, and sneak into his secret room once more.

The box with Linda Marsh's name on it sits on the floor where I left it, still unopened. I lift the lid to see a stack of manila folders.

I grab the first one and open it.

A photo of Avery flutters out, and I pick it up.

And I remember the photo...and the conversation with my father it inspired.

———

I STAND, *hands in the pockets of my jeans, facing my father. He sits in his plush leather chair behind his massive oak desk. It's his place of power.*

This is the position I assume when he calls me to his office. My hands go into my pockets because I know how much he hates it. He thinks it looks disrespectful. Well, good. I don't respect the fucker. He's made my life hell.

"So this is the girl?" He slides a glossy photo across the desk toward me.

I pick it up, and a small smile spreads across my face. I can't help it when I see her, even in a photo.

Avery Marsh. Gorgeous Avery Marsh. She smiles at me from the two-dimensional image, and it's like she's here, in front of me, her lips curving only for me. She's wearing a blue angora sweater that matches her eyes, and her blond hair falls over her shoulders in those gorgeous waves. I know how they feel beneath my fingers. How soft those lips are when they meet mine.

"You going to answer me?"

"That's Avery Marsh. Yes, she's the one I'm dating."

"Break it off." The three words snap at me like a whip.

I shove my hands farther into the pockets. "No."

Fuck no.

"That wasn't a request, Chance." His voice is deeper and more imposing.

When I was younger, I was afraid. No longer.

"I know. It was an order. A fucking order."

He nods. "Damned right it was, and you will end things with her."

Avery and I have been going out for a while. I've never brought her home to meet my father because I don't want to subject her to him. He's a dick, and I can't stand him. I love her, so why would I put her through that? Especially now that I know exactly how he feels about us being together.

"I will not."

"She's trailer trash, Chance."

Anger boils through me. How dare he? "She lives in a mobile home park. That doesn't make her trash."

He slices his hand through the air. "This discussion is over. You end things with her."

"No. I won't, Dad. I love her."

But my father has gone back to whatever document he was

reading before he summoned me. His gaze is fixed. We're clearly done here.

Fine.

We're done. I walk out. Turn my back on him.

I'll never let Avery go. My father can go fuck himself.

———

DAMN. For almost a year, I thought I'd won that argument. He never bothered me about Avery again.

We—Avery and I—spent as much time together as we could. We held hands in the hallways at school. We attended all the dances and other functions. We made out desperately in my truck, and we talked about going all the way. Avery decided to go on the pill...and then the day came.

That day at the spring.

And the next day, she was gone.

My old man.

My fucking old man. He just waited. He waited until I'd fallen so deeply that I could never return.

And then he took her away from me.

I hope he's rotting in hell.

He must have written the letter. Who else could have? It certainly wasn't me.

I'm still holding the document about Linda Marsh.

And I begin to read.

I scan through the date and the legalese to find the parties to the agreement.

Jonathan Bridger.

And Linda Marsh.

Holy. Fucking. Hell.

21

$\mathcal{A}$VERY

"WE WERE LIVING IN A TRAILER," Mom begins. She grabs a shirt from the laundry basket and starts to fold it. Her hands fumble and she gives up, tossing it back in the pile.

"I know that," I say numbly.

We're still on the service porch, and I'm sitting in an old aluminum lawn chair—one that I think used to sit outside our mobile home on the outskirts of Bayfield. Mom drops across from me in a metal folding chair—the kind that goes with a card table.

I never thought about the fact that we lived in Rainbow Estates—though *estates* was certainly generous.

But to the rest of Bayfield, we were trailer trash. At least that's what Mom is trying to get me to believe.

Funny. I never felt like trailer trash when I was a kid, and no one at school ever made me feel less than. Seems to be my mother's problem.

"I worked my tail off at that factory, and I took whatever odd jobs I could find during the many layoffs."

I remember she was always busy, rarely at home. "I know all this, Mom. I was there."

"I was determined that you wouldn't have to help," she says. "You were a kid."

I have no idea where she's going with this, but so far, none of it is important. "Again, I know this."

"You tried to give me your babysitting money once," she says. "Do you remember that?"

I have to dig deep because I've buried most of my Bayfield memories, but I find it. "Yeah. I remember."

"I didn't take it. I told you to get yourself something."

I did. I got myself a chocolate malt in town and a pair of fake pearl earrings. I loved those earrings. I was going to wear them to the prom with Chance...

"Anyway," Mom continues, "things were looking bleak your senior year. They closed down the factory."

I widen my eyes. "I know it closed down, but that was after we moved." The puzzle pieces begin to link together. "Wait. Is that why—"

She sighs and holds up a hand. "Let me get this out, Avery. This isn't easy for me."

I sigh. "Fine. Go ahead, Mom."

"I wasn't sure if we were going to make it. I was behind on rent, and the car was on its last legs. I remember thanking God every time you went out with Chance Bridger, because I knew you'd get a decent meal."

"Mom, I never went hungry."

She inhales. "I know you didn't. I made sure of that."

I regard my mother. She's got a few wrinkles around her mouth and around her eyes, but she's still very attractive. She's kept her figure, and her cheeks are always rosy. But when I think back—

She was always pretty, but she got thin for a while.

Almost too thin.

And I never went hungry. Oh, God.

"But you did, didn't you? *You* went hungry, Mom."

She nods, swallowing. "Sometimes. Just that last year. It was more important for you to eat."

How could I have missed my mother fading away before my eyes?

Easy. I was in love. First love, true love.

"You were a child, Avery. Don't punish yourself for what you failed to notice. It was fifteen years ago. Besides..."

"Besides what?"

She clears her throat. "You may not feel any guilt at all once you hear the whole truth from me."

My blood chills in my veins. What whole truth? Sure, I know Chance didn't write that Dear Jane letter, but what else could my mother be keeping from me?

"Like I said, I was worried. Money was scarce, and—"

Adolescent feet clomp in the distance, and the screen door opens. "Mom? Grams? I thought we were going out to dinner. I'm starved."

Grady.

He ambles toward us, his tall and lanky frame so much like Chance's at that age. And that hair. That fiery auburn hair...

"What's going on?" He glances between us.

"We're just talking," Mom says.

"Can you talk at dinner? Mom said we were going out."

Ah, to be a teenage boy, with a life that revolves around constantly filling your stomach.

"I did say that." I force a smile. "Go wash your hands. Grandma and I will be right out."

He holds his palms out. "Already done."

"Homework?" I ask.

"All done too. My stomach's a tomb, Mom." He pats his belly.

I gaze at my mother. Whatever she's keeping from me will have to wait. My son—and his appetite—comes first.

And then an ice pick spears my heart.

My son is hungry, and I have the means to feed him.

My God, what would I do if I couldn't? What must my mother have felt? The fear that she might not be able to feed her child?

And oh my God...

What did she do to make sure I'd never go hungry?

And I know, as if I've always known.

No aunt died, leaving us money.

I look to my mom. She doesn't say a word but I can read it on her face. Being back in Bayfield has given me a closer sense to how things were.

To feed her child, my mother entered into a deal with the devil himself.

Jonathan Bridger.

22

HANCE

I SIT on the dusty floor, stunned, staring at the words on the document.

Five hundred thousand dollars. Half a million dollars for Linda Marsh to leave town and take her daughter with her.

Not only that, but another fifty thou each year she stayed away. Kept Avery away from here. From me.

I shake my head. I don't remember a lot about Linda Marsh. She worked odd hours and Avery and I did our share of making out in their mobile home. We couldn't make out at my place. My old man made it clear how he felt about Avery.

Plus? I didn't like being home. I missed my mother.

God, my mother…

Without looking at the rest of the contents of Linda's box, I push it aside and scour the small room, tossing more boxes until I find it. The one I knew would be there.

Lisabeth Davies.

My mother. She was tall and gorgeous with hair the color of a Montana sunset. I last saw her the summer I turned thirteen. She cried when she left, told me she loved me, said she'd be back for me as soon as she could.

I believed her for a while. I believed my beautiful mother would return and get me out of my bastard father's house.

But she didn't. She never came. I never saw or heard from her again.

I grew to hate her, and then I met Avery. Avery, who taught me how to love again. That someone would stick around for me. To be mine to keep always. Unconditionally.

Until she, too, left. Walked away without a word just as my mother had.

And ripped my heart to shreds.

"Why'd you stay at the ranch?" Austin asked me a

couple nights ago when we were sharing a beer on the deck.

"Because this ranch saved me," I told him. "When Avery disappeared, I threw myself into ranch work. I couldn't leave. This place was like a person to me. My savior, in a way."

"Even though our father was here?" he wondered. He never met Jonathan Bridger but hates him just as fiercely.

"In spite of that," I added. "I had nothing to do with him, not once I turned eighteen. I even moved out of this house. I only moved back after he died."

The box is light. I rip off the lid and—

The only contents are a death certificate.

I pick it up and scan it.

A tear falls from my eye. It's dated a week after she left.

I shake my head. My mother didn't leave me. She died. Cause of death is listed as...

Suicide.

My mother wasn't suicidal.

Was she?

Living with Jonathan Bridger could drive anyone to the brink. What was different about her? Why did my father keep her around longer than his first two wives? He dumped Austin's mom when she was pregnant. Same, as far as I remember, with Miles's mom. Why did he keep me here, but abandon his first two sons? I fear I may never know the answers to those questions.

And why, after all these years, did he bring them back here when he died?

He never met them once. Why force them to a ranch that they'd never seen? To become Bridgers in more than name?

I scoff. The answer to that last question is simple. To fuck me over. To pit us against each other.

My father knew I hated him. He didn't give a shit. He probably knew Austin and Miles didn't like him much either. It wasn't as if they came knocking and wanting to play catch when they were young. No. They stayed away until a will forced them back.

And dear old Dad didn't set up the paperwork out of the goodness of his heart. He didn't have one. He did it so Austin and Miles would come here. Hate the place. Hate me. Leave so that the will went to shit. So they had the money in their hands but let it slip through their fingers. A billion dollars would be lost.

At least we're having the last laugh on that. I love my brothers, and 'I know they feel the same way. Sure, we give each other shit, but isn't that what brothers are supposed to do?

I run my hands over the death certificate.

At least now I know why she didn't come back. She couldn't.

"I'm sorry, Mom," I say out loud. "I'm sorry for your pain."

I shove the death certificate back in the box and toss it aside. I have to process her death somehow, but now isn't the time. She's gone. Has been for almost twenty years. But Avery's back and I need to know the truth. All of it. Back to Linda's box.

The rest of the file folders contain ledgers showing how much my father shelled out to Linda over the years to keep Avery away from me. He paid for her college. For Avery's. He bought them a house in a suburb of Phoenix. All this to keep me from the love of my life.

Because he thought she wasn't good enough for me.

"That's a load of shit," I say, again out loud. "It had nothing to do with Avery. He just didn't want me to be happy."

He just wanted to be an asshole and see me suffer. I grew too big for him to physically control me. This way he could destroy me without raising a finger. Fucking bastard.

"I'll see you in hell," I mutter.

I rise, brush off my jeans.

Avery's been gone less than a day, but even that's too much.

Now that I know so much kept us apart, it's time to put the past behind us. All of it.

Time to fly to Phoenix and get my woman.

But then my gaze falls on a different box with a name scrawled in thick black marker on the top—the only one marked in that way.

Grady Landon Marsh.

Never heard of him. He must be some relative of Linda's. Someone else my father paid off, probably.

I shove it to the side.

I don't have time for more of my father's nonsense. I need to bring my woman home.

23

 VERY

WATCHING my son put away a thirty-ounce porterhouse makes me smile. Truly smile. This kid is everything to me. I live for this child. Only him, until now. I' thought he would be the only guy in my life with Chance out of it, but now... I want Chance, too.

If only things could be different. Chance will never forgive me for keeping his son from him. From watching him grow, learn, turn big enough to eat an entire side of cow in one sitting.

"You two have any room for dessert?" I ask, holding my stomach. I don't think I need to eat for another week.

"Not me." Mom pats her mouth with a napkin.

"Of course. I'll have the chocolate cake." Grady chews on the end of the T-bone.

"I don't know where you put it." Mom shakes her head with a smile. "To be young again."

Our server comes by, and Grady orders his cake.

"Anything for you ladies?" He aims his grin squarely on me.

"A cup of coffee," I say. "Black."

"Same." Mom smiles. Once he's gone, she says to me, "He was checking you out, Avery."

I roll my eyes. "He's got to be ten years younger than I am."

"I'm not telling you to go out with him. I'm just remarking that he finds you attractive."

"Gross," Grady says with an eye roll.

"Your mother is a beautiful woman, Grady." Mom straightens the silverware on her empty plate.

"She's a mom." Grady downs the rest of his soda. As if moms can't be pretty. Or dateable.

The server comes back with the cake, which Grady inhales. I take a few sips of the mediocre coffee. I nod to Mom. "You ready?"

I want to get home and get mom to tell me the rest of what she was going to say before Grady interrupted us. I know it's important and a secret she's kept for years.

She twists her lips. "Yes. Let's go."

———

GRADY BARRELS inside and heads to his room to play video games. I sit down on the couch, slouching so my feet can rest on the coffee table.

"Avery..." Mom begins, standing behind a matching chair and holding the back.

"Yes. I know. Let's talk."

She looks around. "Not here."

I frown. "Why not? Grady's in his room. He won't hear us."

Most houses in Phoenix are one story because of the heat. The cost is too great to keep a second story cool. Ours is like that. Still, Grady's room is down a long hallway at the back of the house. If he's playing video games as he planned, he's got a headset on and 'wouldn't know if a bomb went off three feet behind him.

She sighs and takes a seat on the couch next to me. Very close. "Okay. You're probably right."

I turn my head and study her closely as if she's a suspect I'm interrogating. I know her tells better than any criminal's. Or do I?

"Level with me. There was no aunt who left you money, was there?"

She sinks her head into her hands.

Yeah, I figured it out. In fact, now that I know, it all seems so clear. I just didn't notice at the time because I was heartbroken over Chance, and then hormonal with the pregnancy. Nearly losing my life delivering Grady put things in a new perspective for me. Chance was gone, but Grady was here, and he needed me. He became my life, and I buried the past.

Mom finally lifts her head. Her eyes are bleak. "I'm sorry."

"Did Jonathan Bridger come to you? Or did you go to him?"

She purses her lips and swallows hard. "It's not that simple."

"Sure it is. Who made the first step?"

"He did," she says. "But the first time he came to me I told him to go fuck himself."

I jerk forward, drop my feet to the floor. "Wait a minute. This wasn't a one-time thing?"

She shakes her head. "He didn't want you with his son, Avery, and he was willing to pay a lot of money to break the two of you up."

I know that, but it still hurts. It makes no sense. Why do something like that?

"What did he have against us?" I wonder.

"He said we were trash." She sighs. "I'm sorry. I'm so sorry."

"I never felt like trash, Mom. I was thinking that earlier when you were fixating on the mobile home. I never thought about it. I was perfectly happy."

"I'm glad." She pats my knee. "I never wanted you to feel that way."

"I didn't. Not until you started talking about it."

She sighs. "Jonathan Bridger made it very clear how he felt about us. And about you dating his son. But I saw how happy you were, Avery. How happy Chance was. It was so obvious you two were in love. I couldn't give you much, sweetheart, but I could at least give you that. I wasn't going to take you away from your first love."

"Except you did," I say, my words practically a whisper.

She blinks back tears. "You have to understand. I didn't see any other option."

I lean into the back of the couch, let my head rest against the high back. My whole body feels like jelly. God, this has been a long day. Just this morning I woke up in Chance Bridger's bed.

Now I'm home.

And I'm hearing the truth from my mother's lips.

"I'm trying to understand, Mom. We were behind on rent. The factory was closing."

A nod, and then, "Yes. I was going to be out of a job within months."

I close my eyes. Did Bridger have a hand in the factory closing? Anything's possible at this point.

"Look at me, Avery."

"I'm sorry, Mom. This is all so much. And I'm exhausted."

"Please. Look at me."

I open my eyes, force myself to sit up, and meet my mother's gaze.

"I went to Jonathan about a month before we left. I told him about our troubles. I hoped he might help without making us leave. By then it was clear how smitten you and Chance were. But his offer was the same. You and I had to leave town, and you had to sever all ties with Chance."

"I see."

"In return, he agreed to pay me half a million dollars."

I jump to my feet. "Half a million dollars!"

"Avery, quiet!" my mother whispers. "Remember Grady."

Fuck Grady overhearing. A half million dollars?

I plunk back onto the couch. "My God…"

"That half mil was pennies to him, and that's not all. We got another fifty thousand each year we stayed away."

I rub my forehead where a headache is trying to erupt. "Jesus."

"Plus he paid for all your hospital bills. For Grady."

"He *knew* about Grady?"

She nods. "He was Jonathan Bridger. He had all kinds of resources. Of course he knew about Grady."

"But Chance…"

Mom shakes her head. "Resources can *keep* you from knowing about something as well."

I've been with Chance the past few days, and it's blatantly obvious he knows nothing about Grady. About the letter. About anything.

"God. Jonathan Bridger made sure Chance never found out he had a son."

"He did."

"And you went along with all of this? All this time? Why, Mom?"

"I had no choice at that point. I was in too deep. I'd already taken his money and used it to get an education. To get *you* an education."

"It's been years since then."

"That money will get Grady an education when the time comes. He'll be able to go to any college he wants."

"I can pay for college for him. I have a job. A good one. Sure, he'll need scholarships, but I don't need—or want—that money touching Grady in any way."

"It already has," she says forlornly.

It's true. That money has put a roof over his head. Paid for his birth. Paid for him being a secret.

"And the aunt story?"

"Jonathan made it clear I couldn't tell you or anyone where the money had come from. The dead aunt story was his idea, and frankly, I couldn't think of anything better."

"Fuck…"

She takes my hand again, rubs my palm with her thumb. "There's something else, Avery."

"Oh, God. What else could there possibly be?"

She clears her throat. "Part of my agreement with Jonathan was that you would never go after Chance. I had to make sure you stayed put."

"You didn't have to do much. No way was I going to go anywhere near Chance after that letter Jonathan forged."

"Honey," she says. "It was *my* responsibility."

"And I'm saying—" My eyes widen at what she laid down. "No. Mom, no."

She closes her eyes, and two tears squeeze out. "I didn't have any other choice, baby."

"Jonathan Bridger didn't write that letter."

"No, baby. I did." She shakes her head, a sob choking out of her throat. "It was cruel and it broke my heart to be so nasty to you, but I had to make sure you 'wouldn't try to go back. And that's not even the worst part."

I swallow down the nausea that threatens to force itself up my throat. "What else? Nothing can possibly surprise me now."

24

CHANCE

I've never been to Arizona. I've seen pictures. Know all about the cactus and the dry heat. Well, hell. It's nothing like they said.

Austin flies the corporate jet into a private airfield outside of the big city. We left Carly and Sadie back home. Both have to work and we aren't lingering.

Once the attendant lowers the stairway, I make my way out onto the tarmac and wonder if the soles of my boots will melt.

It's a dry heat. Right?

It has to be at least a hundred degrees and not a tree in

sight. Rugged orange and brown mountains are all I can see in the distance.

"Holy fuck," I say as Austin and Miles flank me.

"Shit, it's hot," Miles offers.

"Who can live in this?" Austin glances at the sky. "I thought the sky was blue in Montana, but this? I'm used to rain. All the time."

"We're not staying," I tell them. "If I wanted to become a snowbird, I'd pick Hawaii."

"Good choice," Austin adds. "This togetherness thing is really fucking weird."

Our father's will requires us to remain together for the entire year, including travel. If I came to Arizona solo, the will's rules would be broken and we'd forfeit the billions.

We went to Seattle with Austin when his mom was hurt and when that asshole she hired stole flights from their seaplane company. We didn't stay more than a day because that was when Carly fell over Joey Hopkins's dead body.

There aren't going to be any dead bodies on this trip, and we aren't sticking around. Sweat is already dripping down my back. I'm getting Avery and getting the hell out of here.

We stride to the tiny terminal and find an SUV waiting for us as arranged. Shankle is good for something. I take the driver's seat, Miles takes shotgun, and Austin sits in the back.

"Crank that AC," Austin says.

Miles is already fiddling with the buttons while I start the engine. We don't close our doors until the air is pumping out nice and cold.

I use my phone to map out the directions to Avery's house and pull out. I'm watching the road as we talk.

"At this point, after all the fuckery that's been going on, I shouldn't be all too surprised about the payout."

I updated the guys on the plane about what I learned, and why I was hustling to Phoenix. I've waited long enough, and if Avery's living with her mom and not knowing she had a hand in our separation, I'm going to fix that.

I'm the only one who's told her the truth all along. I've been there for Avery from the start. Ever since high school, she's been the constant. The thing I've wanted. Loved. I gave my heart to her, which meant I would protect her. Cherish her. Possess her.

I've shown her how I can cherish and possess. Now I'll protect.

Even if it's from her mom.

An hour later, through some of the worst fucking traffic, we pull up in front of a ranch house. It's in a subdivision of them, one after the other looking identical.

Stucco, tile roof, one story. There's no grass or greenery anywhere. Yards are made of decorative rock and cactus. I feel like I've landed on the moon. A very hot moon.

"Stay here," I tell the guys.

"Like we'd leave the AC," Miles says.

I smirk, leaving the car running as I hop out.

I ring the doorbell. No answer.

I ring again. Still no answer. I glance around, note that all the houses are quiet. Bikes and a few toys are strewn on driveways down the block, but no one's out. It's too fucking hot. I have to wonder if everyone behaves like vampires, only coming out at night when it's cool.

On Avery's front door is a decorative wreath. Kicked in the corner are a pair of worn cleats, and I wonder if Avery took up a sport. Maybe FBI softball games? Again, at midnight?

"Fuck," I mutter to myself. But it's the middle of the day so I return to the car and settle in.

"Pull up the FBI field office on your phone. Let's head there," I say to Miles.

He nods and fiddles until the phone voice tells me to head south for two blocks.

"It's thirty minutes from here," Miles says. "The map's all red, meaning more fucking traffic."

"If we've come here to sit in traffic all day, we need to stop for a drink. Hit the drive thru or a gas station," Austin orders from the back. "Remind me of this weather when it's December and there's three feet of snow on the ground."

I agree. I'm melting, but I'd rather be buried in snow than sweat to death. If we linger here, we'll turn to fucking dust.

As I head out of Avery's neighborhood, I vow to myself once I get Avery in my arms again, I'm never letting go, and I'm never going to come back.

25

VERY

DEBRIEFING SUCKS. It's not enough that Jarvis and I filed our report, but now we have to sit in a conference room with the higher ups and justify everything we did on the case. At this point, I'm damned glad I didn't take that information off the book from Hayes. Turns out, I didn't need to pull Chance's DNA from Grady's hair strand. Just as well.

I'm on autopilot, answering the questions lobbed at me, while the conversation with my mother last night drones in my head.

———

"Jonathan Bridger didn't write that letter."

"No, baby. I did." She shakes her head, a sob choking out of her throat. "It was cruel and it broke my heart to be so nasty to you, but I had to make sure you 'wouldn't try to go back. And that's not even the worst part."

I swallow down the nausea that threatens to force itself up my throat. How could there be something worse than a mother ruining her daughter's life? "What else? Nothing can possibly surprise me now."

She draws in a deep breath, closes her eyes...and pauses.

"For Christ's sake, Mom. Spit it all out, would you?" My patience is wearing thin, and the huge dinner is like a cannonball sitting in my gut.

"Bridger told me I was on notice. That when I heard from him, I had to be ready to hightail it out of town within twenty-four hours, and I'd better be sure you'd never look back."

"Right." I sigh. "I get it. You had the letter ready. Literally on standby for the guy." I shake my head, wondering how my mother could be so damned harsh and brutal to her own daughter.

My God, the words she used...

It was fun, but it's over. You're good and all, but I can't keep you. You have to know that. I'm a Bridger and you're... well, you're just another pussy I fucked at the spring.

The letter turned to ashes within an hour after I read it. Once Mom and I were on the road, I lit it afire and threw it out the car window.

"I had the letter ready, and once you read it, I knew you wouldn't fight me on leaving. I had Jonathan Bridger's money and hotels booked to get us here to Arizona."

"Did you choose Arizona?"

"No, he did. He knew Chance hated the heat."

"Jeez..." I shake my head. I don't know what to feel. Numbness. Shock. Anger. Betrayal. Sadness. Disappointment. "I have to go to bed."

"Not yet. You have to know everything."

"What the hell else is there?" I rub at my temples, trying to ease the ache, wondering if I'm going to upchuck tonight's expensive dinner all over my living room floor.

"He had the two of you watched, and he chose the day we had to leave."

"Right, you said that—" I drop my jaw. "Oh. My. God. He knew. He fucking knew! He knew Chance and I made love. He waited for me to give his son my virginity, and then he took him away from me!" I rise then, pace across the worn carpeting. "He truly was evil."

"He was, sweetheart." Mom wrings her hands. "And I'm so sorry for my part in all of this."

She could have told me the truth at any point in the last fifteen years. Even last week, when I told her I had to go back to Bayfield for a case. Yet, she didn't. Not once.

I walk to my bedroom and cry myself to sleep.

———

I JERK when my phone buzzes on the table in front of me with a text message.

"Sorry," I mumble.

"It's okay, Marsh," McGuinness says. "We're done here. Good job, both of you."

I look at my phone.

Where are you, kitten?

Chance.

I can't help myself..

I melt.

26

HANCE

I PULL into a loading zone in front of the FBI building downtown. I hop out.

Austin takes my seat. "Call when you're done and we'll swing back to get you both."

He's optimistic to think I might be able to toss Avery over my shoulder and drag her out of a federal building full of law enforcement officers and then fly her out of state on a private plane. I don't think it'll be that easy, but I like his hope.

"Want us to grab you a burger?" he calls.

I turn on the sidewalk as I set my Stetson back on my

head. Sadie mentioned a great fast-food place that had amazing burgers, stacked two, three, or even four high on a bun. While it's something to try, we aren't in town for the hamburgers. At least I'm not.

"I'm good. I'll keep you updated."

He nods, Miles offers a finger salute through the closed window, and they're off.

I stop at the security desk and ask for Avery. Maybe I should have called. Before I left Montana. But my goal isn't changing. I'll find her wherever. As the man calls somewhere in the building, I text her.

Where are you, kitten?

She texts back right away.

At work.

Good. I'm in the lobby.

I see the three dots moving, but then they stop.

"She'll be down in a minute," the security man tells me.

I nod, walk away from security, and lean against the wall near a potted cactus.

Five minutes later, Avery approaches from a bank of elevators beyond the security stiles.

Fuck, she's pretty in her corporate skirt and blouse. Heels, too. Her legs are long and lean and perfect. I remember how they feel around my waist.

"What are you doing here?" she asks, a smile on her

face as she comes into my arms. She's surprised, but not upset.

She lets me kiss her in the lobby of an FBI building. Not how I want to, with a lot of tongue and roaming hands, but anytime her lips are on mine is a win.

I brush my nose with hers and murmur, "I'm here for *you*, kitten. We have things to talk about."

I cup her hip with one hand, stroke her hair with the other. Fuck, she is so pretty. I tell her so.

She blushes and glances around. "Come on." She snags my hand.

After giving the security man my ID and getting a sticker pass that I slap on my shirt, Avery leads me through the security area and to the elevators. Once inside, she pushes the third-floor button.

She stands beside me, although we're not touching. She tips her head toward an obvious camera. Ah. So that's why we're not making out right now.

Once the doors slide open, she leads me through an open-concept office area. It's a vast space of desks, most manned by people working on computers or talking on the phone.

"This isn't like the movies," I say.

She glances over her shoulder at me with a smile. "You expected a shootout?"

"Isn't Arizona where the O.K. Corral was?"

She laughs as she swipes her badge to unlock a door, then holds it open for me. It's my job to do that for my woman, but I'll let it slide here at her place of work.

"It is, but a few hours away by car. Want to play tourist?"

"Too fucking hot," I reply. The building is blissfully cold. Thank fuck.

"I do miss Montana weather," she replies. "Summers are incredible there."

"Then come back with me."

That isn't what I came to talk about, but it's the truth.

Her eyes widen. "You... You want me to move to Montana?"

I step close, but she retreats. I don't stop until she's against the wall behind the door. The room is clearly used for meetings with a table and chairs for six. There are no windows, only bland white walls and overhead fluorescent lighting.

"I want you on the ranch. In my bed. Permanently."

She glances away.

I tip her chin up with my fingers. "Too strong?"

She shakes her head. Licks her lips. "There's something I need to tell you."

I nod, lean in and nuzzle her neck with my nose. Fuck, she smells good. "There's probably a lot we need to talk about. Including why I came all the way here."

She angles her head and clenches the front of my shirt.

"Yes," she breathes.

I cup her breast through her blouse. "Are there cameras in this room?"

She shakes her head, clouding my face with her silky hair. "No."

"Lock the door, kitten."

I pull back enough so she can reach out and flick the lock on the knob. I love that this big, in-charge federal agent obeys me.

"Good girl." I sink back into her, kissing her the way I couldn't in the lobby. "Think you can be quiet?"

We're breathing hard, and I roll my dick into her stomach.

She nods and tugs at my shirt, this time working it from my pants.

I didn't come here to fuck. Hell, I never expected— ever—to get it on in an FBI building. But when have I ever resisted Avery?

Never.

I trace my fingers along her thigh to the hem of her skirt and work it up. By the time I get it around her waist, she's got my jeans open and her hand wrapped around my dick.

"Fuck, Avery."

"Now."

I didn't think we would have tons of foreplay in a conference room, but I barely got my hands on her.

I cup her pussy through her panties and find her hot... and soaked. Thank God. No way would I take her if she 'wasn't ready. I'm big. She's got a tight little pussy and no way will I hurt her.

I hook behind a knee and lift her. She wraps her legs around my waist, and with a quick tug to the side on her panties, I'm buried deep.

My face is buried in her neck, my drawn-out *fuck* stifled by her heated skin.

I thrust into her hard. Deep. Fast.

Clearly, being apart is too much for Avery too. She's running hot and ready and comes on my dick faster than I ever expected. It's a good thing because I don't last five seconds longer.

I'm leaning into her, holding her up because she's boneless in my hold.

A phone rings, and she finally moves.

I set her on her feet as she reaches behind her back and into the rumples of her skirt.

I didn't even notice she had a phone clipped to her skirt even though I walked behind her most of the way through the building.

"Hey, Mom," she says when she answers.

I tuck myself back into my jeans, her eyes on my action. Her mom. Not someone I want in the room, even through the phone, with my dick out. Or Avery's skirt up around her waist. I smooth it down for her as she talks.

"What?" Her eyes are wide and she clenches my forearm with her free hand. "Oh my God! Which hospital?"

Shit. Her mom is hurt. Sick. Something.

"I'll be there in fifteen minutes."

She ends the call. "I have to go. I have to get to the hospital."

As she unlocks the door and pulls it open, reality returns.

"I'll drive," I say, following Avery through the building.

I don't know what's going on, but I'm in this now with her. Good and bad.

She turns, faces me, tears in her eyes. "You can't come with me, Chance." She sniffles. "I'm sorry. We... We have no future. We're done."

27

VERY

"ARE YOU CRAZY?" Chance's eyes look like a madman's as he grabs my shoulders. "I was just inside you, kitten, and now you're telling me we have no future? That you're done? Fuck that. I'm not letting you go. I'm *never* letting you go. I know everything. I know my father kept us apart. I know about the deal he made with your mom. I know everything, kitten, and none of it matters."

But he *doesn't* know everything. He doesn't know that my son—*our* son—is in the hospital.

"It's too late." I pull away from him, run down the

hallway, brushing past Jarvis and his assistant, and knocking a file from his hands. Papers scatter to the floor.

"Marsh?" he says, but I whisk by, Chance in pursuit.

"Bridger?" Jarvis's voice. "What are you doing here?"

Chance doesn't answer Jarvis, and once I'm out in the hallway, racing toward the elevators, one opens. I run inside—

But Chance is too quick. He shoves his arm between the closing doors and enters the elevator. He grips my shoulders again.

Grady. I have to get to Grady. And Chance...

I have to tell him.

He'll never forgive me, but right now, in this desperate moment, nothing matters except my son.

My beautiful son, with hair like wildfire and a personality to match.

"Look at me, Avery."

Chance's voice is stern yet kind, and I can't help myself. I obey him. Like I always have.

I gaze into his gorgeous blue eyes, troubled blue eyes. Troubled because he loves me. And I rebuffed him.

"Don't you dare tell me you don't love me," he says.

"I don't..." I shake my head.

The words won't come. They'll never come, because even when I hated Chance, I still loved him.

I've always loved him.

But he'll never forgive me for keeping him from his son.

He crushes his mouth to mine, and I open for him instantly. Damn the elevator cameras. I don't care—

The doors slide open, and I break the kiss and race through the building to the parking garage across the street.

Must get to my car. To the hospital. To Grady.

Mom didn't have any details when she called me. Only that Grady had been rushed to Mt. Sinai in an ambulance after a car hit him while he was skateboarding during his lunch period.

My fault. All my fault. I should have never let him have that damned skateboard. The first day after his suspension ended too. I should have never...

I press my key fob to unlock my car, but strong hands —gentle, strong hands—pry it from my grasp.

"I'll drive."

"You don't know where you're going," I gulp out.

He pulls out his phone. "You tell me."

I try to swallow down the lump in my throat. "Mt. Sinai."

He taps on his phone. "All set." He opens the passenger side door for me, and I slink into the seat. Sweat makes my blouse cling to my skin.

He's taking over. For now, anyway.

And bless him for it.

He doesn't force me to talk on the way to the hospital, for which I'm grateful. I'll be forced to talk to him soon enough.

All I care about is Grady. I don't know if he's alive or dead at this point.

God, please spare my son. I'll give Chance up. I'll give everything up. Just spare my son.

When Chance pulls into the ER, I dash out of the car without a word to him and run inside.

"My son," I gasp to the receptionist on duty. "Grady Marsh. He was brought—"

"Avery!" Mom races toward me.

I turn. "Mom! What's going on?"

She grabs my hands in hers. "They took him to get an MRI."

"Why aren't you with him?" I demand. My heart is clamoring against my chest and the cool air of the hospital is giving me chills.

"He said he could go by himself."

Of course. He's fourteen, and he thinks he can do everything.

But that means he's conscious and alert.

"They think he probably has a concussion," Mom continues. "He has stitches on his forehead and on his shoulder. A pretty deep gash, but they were able to stop the bleeding and get him stitched up."

I turn to liquid and I fall against my mother. "Concussion?"

"Yes. He's been throwing up, and he lost consciousness—"

"What?" I gasp, freaked all over again.

"He lost consciousness for a few minutes in the ambulance, but he's awake now."

"God, is he in pain?"

"They gave him something for it."

I blink, worried at what it is. "They gave him meds without my permission?"

"It was an emergency, Avery." She pats my hand. "They had the right. And I was here. I told them to do what they had to do to help him."

"Right. Right." I sniff into my mother's shoulder.

I'm both angry at my mother and so very grateful to her. I don't know what to feel anymore. All I know is I have to see my son.

"Avery."

Chance's voice. He's here. Even if I didn't hear him, I could feel him. That safe place. That protective presence. Yet I stiffen and panic.

"What's going on?" he asks. "I thought your mother..."

Mom lets go of me and approaches him. "Hello, Chance."

"Mrs. Marsh." He takes off his hat and nods at her. "What's going on here? Avery said you were in the hospital."

Mom lifts her eyebrows. "She did?"

"I didn't say anything, Chance." I sniffle. "You heard me ask which hospital while I was on the phone. With Mom."

"Then who is—"

A woman in green scrubs interrupts us. "Mrs. Marsh?"

Mom and I both turn.

The woman smiles. "Grady's back from the MRI. He'd like you to sit with him."

Mom turns, but I stop her. "I'll go."

I walk with the woman until we're out of Chance's earshot. "I'm Avery Marsh, Grady's mother. How is he?"

"I'm Dr. Park," the woman says. "I'm the ER resident on your son's case. We're waiting for his MRI results, but unless there's a brain bleed—which is unlikely, given Grady's symptoms—he's going to be just fine after a few days of rest."

Relief courses through me, but I'm in full-on mother mode and won't be happy until I see Grady. And hug him. "Can I take him home? After we get the results?"

"We'd like to keep him overnight for observation. Any

time a patient loses consciousness with a concussion, we like to be extra careful." She smiles. "But that's no reason to worry."

We're walking through the ER, whisking by the curtained-off areas.

"I'm his mother. I'm going to worry."

Dr. Park smiles again. "I know." She pulls back the curtain to reveal a hospital bed...and Grady.

I rush to his bedside. "Sweetheart, are you all right?" I hold back tears at the sight of the stitched-up gash marring his handsome face. He's still my sweet boy.

"I'm okay, Mom," he says, his voice slightly hoarse. "I love you."

"I love you too, baby." I take his hand and sit down on the edge of the gurney. "I'm not leaving your side."

She frowns and glances down at our joined fingers. "I'm sorry. I know you hate the skateboard."

I want to shake him for not listening to me, and now, after getting hurt, he tells me I was right all along. "For good reason."

"You were very lucky," Dr. Park says. "I've seen much nastier skateboard accidents."

"Who hit you?" I demand. "I'll sue the shit out of them."

"It was an accident, Mom," Grady says, yawning.

"We have the name and address of the young woman

driving the car," Dr. Park says. "She stopped immediately and helped Grady. She feels terrible, and the police cited her for reckless driving. But Grady admits he wasn't watching where he was going."

"Still—"

"She insisted on coming to the hospital and she stayed with him until your mother arrived," Dr. Park continues.

The protective lioness in me wants to pummel her, but love and gratitude that my son is okay overrides it quickly. Accidents do happen, especially with reckless boys. And Grady is reckless. Testosterone and a fourteen-year-old boy can be a lethal combination.

"I'll stay with him tonight," I say.

"Mom..."

"Sorry, no negotiation."

An orderly dressed in blue scrubs peeks in. "I'm here to move Grady to his room."

"All right." Dr. Park regards Grady sternly. "This is where we part ways. You listen to your doctors. And to your mother."

"Yes, ma'am," Grady says sleepily.

I hold tight to his hand as the orderly begins moving the hospital bed on wheels.

I'm never letting go.

28

HANCE

"ALL RIGHT, LINDA," I say to Avery's mother once Avery disappears around the corner in the ER. "Start talking. I found a file in my father's office regarding someone named Grady Landon Marsh. Is that who's back there?"

Linda's aged since I saw her last. We all have. Fifteen years 'haven't hurt her too much. She's tanner than I remember. A few extra wrinkles and a few extra pounds. But she looks more worried than she did when she was reassuring Avery.

"This is something you'll have to talk to Avery about, Chance," she tells me.

"Avery's not here," I say. "And you owe me answers, Linda. I found the agreement between you and my father. I think it's time you give me some of the truth. Starting with who Grady is."

Her eyes, so like Avery's, are sunken and sad. "If you found your father's files, then you know who Grady is."

"I didn't look at that file," I say. "I was too fucked up after looking at the contractual agreement you made with my father that separated me from Avery. He paid you off, Linda. He fucking paid you off. At your daughter's expense. And mine."

"I don't expect you to understand."

"I understand you took Avery away from me. God, I love her. I did then. I do now. I always have. I can't believe you'd be that cruel to your own child. If you didn't like me, fine, but Avery? Her heart's so fucking pure. What's worse, you did it by conspiring with my father. Why, Linda? Why would you do that?"

It's hard not to raise my voice in the ER lobby.

"Really, Chance?" She sighs. "Are you so jaded by your riches that you have no idea why I might have made an agreement with your father?"

"I had money. I was eighteen, though barely. I could have gotten money for you. For Avery."

I'm angry, but the truth is, I didn't have any money. My father made sure he controlled all the money from the ranch. And once Avery was gone, I didn't give a shit about the money anyway.

Linda must have been desperate.

Still, I'm angry.

"Who's Grady, Linda?"

Linda shakes her head, running her hands over face. "You need to—"

"Talk to Avery. I know. Avery's not here, and whoever Grady is, he's important enough to make Avery—"

I stop mid-sentence.

Oh, God.

Linda finally straightens up and meets my gaze. "Grady is Avery's son."

I rise, pace, sit back down, rise and pace some more.

So Avery has a child. A son. We'll deal with it. I'll be a good stepfather, and she and I can have more children. Except...

I sit down, face Linda. "Is the father in the picture?"

She shakes her head. "No, Chance."

Poor Avery. A single mom. Well, no longer. I'll take care of her and her son. I'll even take care of Linda.

"I'm back."

I look up. The sweet voice of my love. Her cheeks are tear-streaked, her hair is mussed, and her skirt rumpled. Still, she's the most beautiful thing I've ever seen.

"Avery..." Linda begins.

"They've moved him to a room. They're going to watch him overnight."

"The MRI results?" Linda asks.

"The radiologist is reading them now. We don't know yet, but the doctor is optimistic." Avery holds out her hand to me. "Come with me. I need to talk to you."

"It's okay, kitten. I know he's your son."

Avery glares at her mother, and then turns back to me. Studies my face. "If you're this calm, you clearly don't know everything. Please."

I rise and take her hand. She leads me out of the ER waiting area and then outside in the wretched heat to a wooden bench. She sits down and pats the space next to her.

I take the seat, and then she takes both of my hands in her small ones.

"Chance, I'm sorry," she admits. She studies my chin and then finally meets my gaze.

"For what? For having a son?"

She gulps. "God, no. He's the most precious thing in my life. I'm sorry that—" She chokes back a sob.

"Hey." I squeeze her hands. "He's okay. He's going to be okay."

She nods, gulping again. "Chance, I—"

"Listen," I say, "it's all okay. I know what my father did. I know about the agreement between him and your mother. He was a vicious and evil man, but he's gone now, and I swear to God he'll never hurt us again. I'll take care of you. You, your mother, and your son, kitten. You're all mine now."

She sniffles. "Oh, Chance. You really don't see, do you?"

"See what?"

"Grady. God, when you see him…" She inhales. "He's yours, Chance. Grady is your son."

My body goes numb. Completely numb. It's hot as fuck out with the sun beating down on us but I don't feel it.

No. Avery Marsh did not just tell me I have a son. A son that she kept from me for—oh my fucking god—fourteen years. A teenager?

My jaw drops, and I want to say so much. Emotion rolls through me. Anger. Rage. Frustration. Resentment.

Disbelief.

"You were on the pill," I finally eke out.

She nods. "I was. I wasn't lying to you, Chance. I swear. I don't know what happened. It had only been a month, and maybe it just didn't work for me. Or I missed a dose. You had super swimmers. Whatever. I was barely eighteen. And I…"

I rise then, my hands clenched into fists. For fifteen years she left me in the dark about this. "Fuck you. Fuck you and your mother and most of all, fuck my father. Where is he? Where is my son?"

She sobs into her hands. "They moved him to a room."

"Which room?" I grit out. "Which fucking room?"

She swallows. "Room 506, but he doesn't know you, Chance, and he's on meds for the pain, and—"

I walk forward, resentment fueling me, back inside where I stride through the ER and into the main hospital. I find the elevators and wait for one to open. Once it does, I step inside and push the button for the fifth floor.

I'm focused. Determined. I need to see my child.

Holy shit. My son.

Only then do I realize I have no idea what to say to this boy.

I sink my head into my hands, and I do something I haven't done since Avery left me.

I fucking cry.

The elevator doors open on the fifth floor, and I pull myself together and walk into the pediatrics wing. Nurses and orderlies are bustling around, and I walk through the wing, eyeing each room number.

500

502

504

Then—

506

The door is cracked, and I peek in. Linda sits in a chair by the bed, but from this angle I can't see the boy.

I step back.

Avery is right. He doesn't know me. He has a concussion, and the last thing he needs is some stranger storming into his room.

I wipe the sweat from my brow.

And then I leave.

———

"What do you mean you just left?" Miles demands.

The three of us are at a restaurant having dinner. Rather, they're having dinner. Even after having burgers, they're eating again. I can't. My stomach is rolling with nausea.

"What was I supposed to do? I'm a stranger to the kid. And Avery..." I rake my fingers through my damp hair. Fuck, it's hot here. Even inside.

"I understand where he's coming from," Austin says, poking a piece of broccoli with his fork.

"I fucking don't," Miles counters. "That's your kid in there. And your woman."

I take a drink of my scotch. It's a scotch kind of evening. "The kid has a possible brain injury. He doesn't need a long-lost father showing up."

How could she keep him from me? After the way we reconnected in Montana... I thought there weren't any secrets left. They just keep on coming.

"You haven't heard her side of it, man," Austin says.

"I've heard all I need to hear." I take another drink. "I would have been there for her. I would have done anything for her and the kid."

"But she didn't know that, Chance," Austin says. "All she knew was that letter."

"Goddamned letter." I polish off my scotch and wave to our server, holding up the glass.

He nods and heads to the bar.

"Easy," Miles says. "You're not a drunk, Chance."

I frown. "Tonight may change that."

The server brings my drink and sets it in front of me.

"He's cut off," Miles says to the server.

"Fuck you," I grit out.

"Take it out on me," Miles says. "I can handle it. Just don't take your anger and frustration out on booze. Or on your woman."

"Do you love her?" Austin asks.

"I've always loved her," I easily admit. "I never stopped. Even now, I'm mad as hell, but I still want to grab her and kiss her. Protect her from everything."

"You can still do that. For her and your son." Austin

glances at his phone. "I need to give Carly a call. Excuse me. Back in a minute."

He slides out of the booth and heads toward the bathroom hallway.

"He's fucking whipped," Miles says, shaking his head.

"And you're not?"

Miles ignores my comment. "You know what I'd do."

"Yeah. You'd march right back to the hospital and take over. That's not my style."

"What *is* your style? To sit back and be a wuss? When we showed up, you were a pain in the ass, ordering us around and being grumpy as fuck. When Avery was there, you were different. Now? You've got a fucking child. You don't abandon things, dude. Especially *your child.*"

I glare at my brother. "You want to take a walk outside?" I curl my hands into fists. "I'll show you which one of us is a wuss."

"Calm down, bro. You're the size of a tank. You can take on an army for sure. That's not the point and you know it."

"You think I should go back."

"Hell yeah. It's what I'd do." He finishes his scotch, clearly stopping at one. "You don't have to freak the kid out. But you should see him. You should see Avery. Make it clear you're there for both of them."

"I love her," I murmur.

"Does she know that?"

I nod. "Yeah. I told her. She hasn't said it back."

"Is that going to stop you from taking what's yours? Because no matter how much scotch you drink, you've got a full-on family now."

I rise, leaving my second scotch untouched. "Hell, no, it's not."

29

VERY

Mom went home, and I'm lying in the recliner in Grady's room on the pediatric floor, one of his hands in mine.

The MRI results were negative. No brain bleed. Just a mild concussion, and Grady should recover completely within ten to fourteen days. Until then, no skateboarding or other activity. No screen time. Loud music.

Frankly, I'd love to keep him off the damned skateboard for life, but I promised I'd never be that kind of mother—the kind who doesn't let her kid fly. Bumps and bruises—and concussions, in this case—are a part of life. I'm thrilled it wasn't any more serious.

Except we're getting him a helmet and I'm going to glue it to his head.

Grady is sleeping soundly, but I can't help checking his pulse every now and then. He's hooked up to machines that will alert his nurse if anything goes awry, but she's not his mother. I am.

I'm about ready to drift off myself—what a day—when a knock sounds on the door.

"Yes?" I say.

The nurse doesn't usually knock.

The door opens.

Chance—big, strong, muscular—walks in holding a bouquet of something I don't recognize.

"Hi, kitten."

My heart lurches at the sight of him, then I start to worry. This is the moment I've been dreading... forever. Will he take Grady away? "What are you doing here?"

"I shouldn't have run off. I'm sorry." He clears his throat and glances at Grady. "And I didn't come up here earlier. I mean, I did, but I didn't come into the room. He—" Chance glances at our sleeping son. "He doesn't know me. And...I didn't want to scare him."

"He's sleeping, Chance. He needs his rest."

"I know. I don't want you to wake him." Chance sets the flowers down and walks toward Grady. Stares down at him in awe. "Damn. That red hair."

"You sure can't claim he's not yours," I say.

He glares at me. "I would never!"

"Shh. Don't wake him. And..." I sigh. "I'm sorry. That was uncalled for."

"It sure was. All of this has been uncalled for. Why didn't you tell me?"

"The letter," I murmur.

He tugs off his hat and runs a hand over his head. "That fucking letter."

I still can't believe my mother wrote it. That Jonathan Bridger forced her hand the way he did.

Chance pulls up a chair and sits at Grady's bedside. He fingers a lock of his son's red hair. "He's beautiful, Avery."

I nod. "He is. He's everything to me."

"He is to me too. Now that I know he exists."

Without meaning to, I choke out a sob. "I'm so sorry."

"I didn't come here to yell," Chance says. "Or to make you feel guilty. I'll never understand how all this happened to us. How my old man could be such an unfeeling sociopath, playing around with people's lives."

I say nothing.

"If I'd known..." He shakes his head.

"Your father fixed it so you'd never know," I tell him. "My mom told me everything."

"How could a father hate his own son so much?" Chance looks at the ceiling.

"It wasn't you he hated. It was me, Chance. He didn't want us together. He thought I was trash."

"He *was* trash, but I knew the man. He didn't hate you, Avery. Who could hate you? He didn't know you. All he knew was that you made me happy, and he took you away from me because of that alone."

I don't have the stamina to argue the point. While I agree that Jonathan Bridger had no love for his son, I also believe he didn't want his son with the likes of me. What does it even matter at this point? It is what it is.

I glance at the flowers. They're odd, and something I've never seen. The bright orange blooms look like they'd be more at home on the head of a tropical bird than in a bouquet. "What are those?"

He chuckles. "Ugly, aren't they? They're called birds of paradise. You're supposed to bring flowers when you come to the hospital, but what the hell kind of flowers do you bring to a guy? So I went into the gift shop downstairs, and this is what they suggested."

"You didn't have to. Grady hates flowers."

"So did I at his age," he replies. "Damn. I know absolutely nothing about my own son."

Words catch in my throat. He's right. He doesn't.

"Tell me about him, kitten."

"He's got a good heart. And he's great at sports. Basketball and football are his favorites. He's smart. Loves science and math. And he loves that damned skateboard. And video games. He's stubborn and muleheaded, like someone else I know."

Chance smiles. "I used to love basketball and football."

"I know. I was there."

"But I hate video games."

"He may look like your clone, but he's his own person. He's not going to be a carbon copy of you."

"I know that." Chance finally removes his Stetson and places it next to the vase of flowers on the counter along the far wall. "Avery, tell me what to do. How do I make this right?"

"We can't go back to the past, Chance."

"Why the hell not? I have everything, Avery. I can give the two of you a good life. You'll live on the ranch. Your mom too. I'll teach Grady everything I know."

"He's a city kid, Chance. What if he hates the ranch? What if he hates small-town life?"

"He's a kid. He'll go where you tell him to go."

I sigh, and a yawn splits my face. "Go home, Chance."

"Avery..."

"Please. Just go."

"But I love you, kitten. I fucking love you. I never stopped."

I love you too, Chance. I never stopped either.

I want to say the words so badly, but they hover on my lips, never quite materializing.

"I had to move on, Chance. If I hadn't, every time I looked at our son would have been painful for me. He needed me. He needed me whole."

"Are you saying you don't love me? That it's him or me and never *us?*"

I don't reply.

"Those kisses. That lovemaking. You love me. I felt it."

Sadness sweeps through me, and my heart smashes into pieces. Chance won't want me when he finds out I can't give him anymore children. It's better to end it this way.

"You can get to know Grady if you want to," I say.

"Damn right, I will, but Avery, I want *you* too."

"Please, Chance." I will my voice not to break into sobs. "Just go home. Once Grady is recovered, we'll figure something out."

———

THE NEXT DAY IS SATURDAY, and Mom picks Grady and me up from the hospital. We get him settled in his room with his video games, but with the sound turned off, no headset, and only for a few minutes.

I sit down at the kitchen table with a magazine, and Mom brings me a cup of coffee.

"What are you doing, Avery?"

"Reading *Cosmo*. What does it look like I'm doing?"

"I mean with Chance. Why'd you send him away?"

He did as I requested and left. I cried most of the night, wishing things could be different.

"You know why."

"He loves you. After all these years he never found anyone else, and neither did you."

"I tried."

"You did, but Tyler saw through the façade and figured out what I've always known. You're in love—you've always been in love—with someone else."

I close the magazine and trail my finger over the model on the glossy cover. Models always look so sullen these days. She looks how I feel.

"I am," I admit. "Being with him again was everything. But Grady is also everything, and I... I took fourteen years of Grady away from him, and I can't give him another child. He deserves to be there for the birth of a child, to carry him or her around on his shoulders, to teach a kid how to dribble a basketball. To ride a horse." I close my eyes. "He would have been a great dad."

"He'll *be* a great dad. To Grady. And for God's sake,

Avery, if he wants more children, the two of you can adopt."

My phone buzzes then. "It's Jarvis. I should take this."

"On a Saturday?"

"The FBI waits for no one." I put the phone to my ear. "Hey, Jarvis."

"Hey, Marsh. How's Grady?"

"Home and on the mend. He'll be annoying me within a few hours, bored."

"I guess then you haven't you checked your email?"

"Not yet."

"We've got a new assignment. In Dallas. We leave Monday morning."

Dallas? "I can't do it. Grady needs me."

"I thought you brought him home today."

"I did. But…"

He's healing well, and Mom is here. Maybe a new assignment is just what I need.

"All right. I guess I'll see you at the airport Monday." I end the call.

"The airport on Monday?" Mom asks.

"Assignment in Dallas."

"Another? So soon? You sure it's the best time?"

I sigh. I'm not sure of anything anymore.

My mother gets into my face then. She doesn't play the mom card a lot, but I see it coming.

"You listen to me, Avery Lee Marsh. You are getting on a plane to Montana tomorrow morning. You're going to Bayfield, and you're going to tell Chance you love him."

"Mom—"

"No buts. I had a hand in separating you two all those years ago, and damn it, I'm not going to sit idly by and let you give up on this second chance. Grady's in good hands with me."

"I know that, Mom. But..."

"What did I just say? You're taking a decision away from Chance. The decision to be with you even if you can't give him more children. I had a hand in keeping him from Grady, and I won't let this happen a second time. Let him decide, Avery. You tell him you love him, and you let *him* decide."

30

CHANCE

"FUCK, man, I can't feel my shoulders."

Miles stands in the barn, sweat dripping down his brow. His shirt is as soaked as mine. He rubs a shoulder and winces.

"Yeah, I can't throw any more bales of hay. Fuck, you make me feel old."

Austin's right there with him, grumbling about today's chores.

We flew back from Arizona late last night. There was no reason to linger. With Austin as our pilot, all we had to do was log a flight plan and we were out of there.

Miles and Austin weren't happy with me leaving.

I wasn't happy in general.

So to numb my mind in work, I chose stacking hay bales as our task.

It's hard work, but it needs to be under cover so it doesn't mold and rot. So now there's stacks of it in the barn for the animals.

"Whatever," I say, grabbing another bale and tossing it up onto the stack. Loose bits of hay fly through the air.

Miles sneezes.

"Look. I didn't take you for a masochist," Miles says.

"What the fuck are you talking about?"

"You left your *family* in Arizona. Why the hell would you do that?" he pushes.

"Then you want to toss hay bales as penance?" Austin adds.

"These need to be stored for the winter. It's not like I'm looking for shit jobs to do."

"Really? We can fix the porch railing that Louisa's been telling us about."

Austin has a point.

"Or we can have one of our hands do all this shit, like normal ranchers," Miles says.

"I don't want to think. I don't want to feel," I admit.

"Well, I'm feeling." Miles winces. "I feel my shoulders and lats fucking screaming."

"Sadie will make it all better with a massage," I tell Miles. "Quit your grumbling."

Miles raises his hands. "No. You quit yours. You want to blow up your life, fine. But I'm not suffering for it."

"I didn't blow up my life!" I yell. "My father did when he paid off Avery's mom. Avery did when she didn't tell me she was having my baby. When she kept it from me this past week when she was here. I was *fucking* her and she didn't tell me!"

Austin and Miles stand there and stare, wide-eyed. Yeah, I hulked out.

"Fine, she didn't tell you. But you have a child and you haven't even talked to him. Is that what you want to be, an absentee father like Jonathan Bridger?"

I see red and shove Miles for those words.

"I'm nothing like him. None of us are."

"Then prove it," he snarls. "Get your head out of the past and look to the future. You decide what you take from our father. Know what he did, and don't do any of it. Be a man. Be there for your kid." Miles turns and storms out of the barn.

Austin studies me. "He's right. You got the shaft. I'll give you that. But you love her. You love your child, even if you haven't met him. Go get them. Make a life. Give Jonathan Bridger the middle finger by living it with love. With them."

"He's right."

A new voice has me spinning around. A voice I'll always remember.

Avery.

She's here.

31

VERY

I WENT to the main house first and was met by Sadie and Carly. They wanted to pull me inside and talk because they hadn't had any opportunity while I'd been in town for the investigation. They know the truth now. All of it.

Chance told Austin and Miles, who told Carly and Sadie, what happened in Phoenix, and I was thankful I didn't have to catch them up.

There was so much. A nightmare of a story that spanned fifteen years.

They hugged me. I cried, which isn't a surprise since I' cried all the way here. The person beside me on the plane kept giving me weird looks and then bought me a drink from the flight attendant.

That made me cry even more.

Being the romantics they are, Sadie and Carly pushed me out the door—never actually letting me go beyond the front porch—and toward the barn where the guys were slinging hay bales.

Equal parts excited and terrified, I made my way there, then inside. I stood in the shadows and listened to Miles and Austin rip into Chance while I ached for him.

Of course he's angry. Of course he's conflicted. I pushed him away. I never told him how I feel. I fucked him in a conference room at work. I told him he had a teenaged child. Mental whiplash.

I couldn't leave him like this a second longer, so I spoke up.

And he turned.

And there's the man I love.

"Where's Grady?" he asks.

"With my mom."

"He's okay?"

I nod. "Yeah. He'll be fine." I look around. Miles and Austin have vanished.

"What are you doing here?" he asks.

I swallow.

"You pushed me away. I left."

A tear slides down my cheek and he steps close and groans at the sight. With his dusty fingers, he swipes it away.

"Don't cry. Fuck, I can't stand it when you cry."

"It's my own fault. I've messed everything up."

"No. My father did. Your mother."

I nod.

"I drove you away instead of telling you the truth."

He cups my jaw and I meet his eyes. The ones that could always see into me.

"I love you, Chance."

A groan rips from him.

"I do. I always have. I never stopped. I didn't tell you about Grady because of the letter. Then I didn't tell you last week because I didn't trust you. No, I didn't trust *us*. I was afraid you'd take him from me."

His eyes flare wide.

"Never."

"I... you were so angry. Rightfully so. What would keep you from taking him? I mean, you have the means. I couldn't fight you."

"You're his mother."

"And you're his father. I've kept you from him."

"You have, but you had your reasons. My brothers told me to stop living in the past. I think they're right."

I nod. I agree.

"You. Me. Grady. We belong together."

"You aren't angry?" I ask.

"Oh, I'm fucking furious so much kept us apart." He slides a lock of hair behind my ear. "But no longer. The best revenge is living a good life. To be loved and love in return."

Tears fall now and I can't stop them. He pulls me into his strong, sweaty embrace.

"That's a lot of tears, kitten."

I pull back and he loosens his hold.

God, how can I tell him this? I gulp. "In the future, I can't... I can't give you more children. Grady's it for us. The delivery was so bad they took my uterus. I—"

He pulls me into his embrace, squeezes me tight. "Oh, my sweet baby. I'm so sorry. I should have been there for you. Helped you through everything."

"You're not...disappointed?"

He put his fingers over my lips. "Only that I wasn't with you when you needed me. God, Avery. The pain that must have caused."

"Oh, Chance..." I sob.

"Shh... I'm not a greedy man. All I ever wanted was you. Now we have Grady too. That's enough. It'll always be enough."

"God, I love you." I get up on my tiptoes to kiss him.

He kisses me back and we get lost in it.

Pulling back, he kisses along my jaw. "Remember when we used to make out in the hay loft?"

I smile through my tears and nod.

"You think if I take you up there, you'll let me go all the way this time?"

I can't help but laugh.

"Maybe."

He pulls me along to the ladder and I climb first. I know he's looking at my ass as he follows me close behind.

Once we're in the loft, he pulls me back into his arms and kisses me. It's like all the years melt away and it's only Chance and me, our whole lives ahead of us. He moves us so I'm pressed against a thick post, one that goes from the ground up to the roof. There, Chance only strips us bare enough to get inside me.

When he plunges deep, my legs wrapped around his waist, I cry out his name. It's the only one I want from my l lips.

"Fuck, sweetheart. I'll never get enough of this. Never want you to leave." He pulls back, fills me again. "You're mine." Again. "I love you." Again. "You're moving here." Again. "Forever."

If fucking me into agreement is his plan, it's working. I want to be with him. On this ranch as we planned all those years ago, under a blanket of stars.

"Yes," I whimper and again he makes me come.

We come together.

He holds me, our breaths ragged, our foreheads touching.

"Marry me."

I clench around him and he growls.

I stroke his face and he lifts his head so his blue eyes meet mine.

"Marry me," he says again.

"This is how you ask me?" I whisper.

A smile tips up the corner of his sweaty face. "I'm inside you. What better place can I be to ask you to be my wife?"

I can't argue, really.

"It's a little late in coming. Fifteen years. I meant it then. I mean it now. Be my wife. Make me the luckiest man."

I blink back tears. Nod.

"Is that a yes?" he asks, his deep voice laced with hope.

"Yes. It's a yes."

He pulls back and thrusts into me again.

"Yes." I say again. And all the while he fucks me again. I've only ever wanted to be Mrs. Chance Bridger. The truth is out. Nothing stands in our way.

Chance is finally mine and I'm his.

Forever.

EPILOGUE

HANCE

"I THINK a shot of the good stuff will calm all our nerves," Miles says, grabbing the bottle of twenty-five year Macallan from the bar.

"Have I taught you nothing?" I grab the bottle from him. "You don't shoot this. You savor it."

"Still," Austin pipes in, "I could use a little something. I can't believe we're all about to become husbands."

"Not what Jonathan Bridger expected when he set up his will, huh?" I asked them.

"Our father can fuck off," Miles said.

"With the DOJ case proving he did everything they

said, it's over. A fine to Bridger Corp and that's it. Pretty hard to put a dead man in jail," Austin says.

Yeah, it's all over. The DOJ found our father guilty, but it didn't go any further than a fine. Whatever. We all left the fucker behind in our minds and hearts.

I take three lowball glasses out of the cabinet and pour one finger, no more, of the scotch into each.

"How do you think the girls are doing?" Miles looks over his shoulder as if he can see them. Which he can't, since they're not here. He's totally whipped. I can't mess with him about it because I am too. All three of us are.

"They're fine," I say. "I just saw Avery and her mom. They said they had a great time at breakfast with Carly, Sadie, and their mothers. It's amazing to me how well they all get along."

"Damned good thing." Miles takes the glass I hand him. "Since they're all going to be living under one roof. At least this house is a ranch-style mansion. But who gets the master suite?"

"Uh...who do you think?" I hand Austin his scotch.

He swirls the amber liquid in the glass. "I don't rightfully care if Chance gets it. Every bedroom in this house has a private bath. In a way, they're all master suites. Besides, once this year is up, I'm going to build a house for Carly and me over on the eastern side of the ranch, where she can be closer to the animals."

"I suppose I can't complain if you take the master," Miles says. "After all, you're the one who had to live with our sire. He screwed us all over, for sure, but you got the worst of it, being separated from your woman for so long, and missing out on your son's first fourteen years."

I take a drink of the smooth liquor, let its smokiness coat my throat. "I'll never forgive him for that. Damn." I shake my head, pushing down the anger and ensuring all I think about is what I have now. "Part of me still can't believe it. I have a son. A fucking son!"

"Grady's a good kid." Austin raises his glass. "And here's to Carly and me giving him a cousin soon."

"Bet I knock Sadie up before you knock up Carly." Miles clinks his glass to Austin's.

"You're on—" But then Austin glances at me. "Shit, Chance. I wasn't thinking. Today's supposed to be happy. We're getting married."

"Yeah, I'm sorry too, bro." From Miles.

"Fuck it." I take another drink. "Today *is* a happy day. So Avery and I won't have more babies. I have the woman I love—who I've always loved—and a son who's my spitting image. Besides, there will still be babies around here. I'll be the doting uncle to all your rugrats." Someone's going to have to teach them not to be such big pussies."

"Yeah, can you believe we're going to stay here? I never

imagined I'd ditch New York for a life in Montana." Miles shakes his head, stunned. He and Sadie agreed he'd settle here. Her job is local and his can be done from anywhere. And the big shop he's been putting together will be the perfect place for his custom work.

As for Austin, there was no decision really for him to go back to Seattle. Carly wasn't going to leave her hometown, not after what happened to her. And Austin's mom will be out of rehab soon and settle here as well. There's enough acreage to build houses for everyone.

I never wanted my long-lost brothers to show up, and now I don't want them to leave.

"Besides," I continue, "who better than their uncle to teach them not to be such big pussies?"

Miles glares at me with a glint of humor in his eyes. "Those are fighting words, little brother."

We all erupt in laughter and polish off our drinks.

I check my watch. "Seems we have somewhere to be, guys."

That's to see my bride. Make her mine legally. Get her in our bed. Just because we can't make any babies sure as hell doesn't mean we can't practice.

AVERY

. . .

MOM, Darla, and Brenda—Carly's and Sadie's mothers, respectively—took over the décor for the vast yard outside the ranch house, and now it's a gorgeous western fairy land with roses and lilies everywhere. Carly, Sadie, and I all wanted a small wedding, so there won't be many guests, but that didn't stop our mothers from going overboard, especially after Chance gave them a blank check.

Somehow, his attorney, Mr. Shankle, was able to secure the release of a bit of the inheritance so we could have a beautiful wedding.

My father has never been in the picture, and Sadie's father is in prison after trying to kill her, so Brenda and Mom will be walking us down the makeshift aisle. Carly's father, Rick Vance, will do the honors for her. Miles and Austin are acting as each other's best men, while Chance —God love him—asked Grady to stand up for him. We women all asked our mothers to stand for us.

Mom fusses with the wreath of baby's breath I'm wearing on my head. "It's just not sitting quite right, Avery."

"It doesn't matter, Mom. I'd be just as happy' if I were marrying Chance in a burlap sack."

I chose a light peach sheath for today, with spaghetti

straps and some unobtrusive beading on the bodice. Sadie and Carly both chose to wear ivory, but with my blond hair and fair skin, white hues wash me out. Sadie's dress has a plunging neckline and flowing skirt that accentuates her curves, and Carly chose a sequined high-neck and bare shouldered number that works well for her petite figure.

"You two look fabulous," Sadie gushes, holding onto her bouquet of white roses.

"You're all so beautiful," Brenda says, blinking back tears.

"I can't believe this day is here." Carly fans herself, practically shaking with excitement. "After everything... I never thought I could be this happy!"

"Stop it." I smile. "You're going to make me cry, and then Mom is going to want to redo my makeup."

"Yes, for goodness' sake, no tears." Mom hands me my bouquet of roses and lilies that match my gown. "You've all come way too far to succumb to tears on this amazing day."

Her involvement in splitting Chance and me apart is still a thing between us. I'm not sure if I'll ever forgive her for it completely, but it proves that love conquers all. She's a good woman who was in a bad spot. With a child almost the same age as I was at the time, I can understand her mother's need to protect. But...

No. I have to look forward, just as Chance and I agreed. My mother loves me and I love her. We don't look back.

Carly swallows, nodding. "I just can't believe I'm this lucky. I found the man of my dreams, and now I have two new sisters as well. I love you both so much."

"You're going to do it, aren't you?" Sadie sniffles. "Avery's right. You're going to make us all cry."

"All of you stop it." Brenda looks at her watch. "Linda is right. You'll smudge your makeup. And it's time, ladies. It's time."

We gather ourselves together and leave the master suite, where we've been getting ready, and walk through the massive house to the French doors leading outside.

A string quartet is playing Mozart, and I peek out at the ornate altar that our mothers put together. The officiant stands ready, and Miles, Austin, Chance, and Grady walk up and take their places.

They're all wearing black pants and white button-downs, no ties. Grady is nearly as tall as Chance, and if possible, his hair is redder.

I close my eyes, holding back tears. I know I'll be crying buckets once I'm saying my vows, but I have to at least get down the aisle.

Darla opens the French doors, where Rick stands to

meet her. Together, they take Carly's arms and lead her toward the altar. And Austin.

Brenda and Sadie are next.

"Are you ready, sweetheart?" Mom asks.

I link my arm through hers. "I've been ready for this moment for fifteen years, Mom."

She gives me a sad smile, then nods. "It was meant to be."

With that, I walk toward my new brothers, my son, and the love of my life.

Fifteen years fades away in an instant, and I'm with Chance at the spring, giving myself to him. That's when I truly gave myself to him. When we made Grady.

Today is simply a formality.

Chance takes my arm from my mother, leans down and kisses my cheek. "You look beautiful, kitten."

I don't trust myself to reply without starting to bawl. I take my place, and I listen as first Austin and Carly, and then Miles and Sadie, recite their vows and exchange rings.

Then the officiant turns to Chance and me.

"Chance and Avery have also decided to write their own vows for today. Chance?"

Chance takes my hand and meets my gaze. "Avery, I dedicated my life to you fifteen years ago. There's never been anyone else for me, kitten, and I bless the fates that brought you back into my life. Thank you for your love, and for my beautiful son."

He glances over his shoulder at Grady, gives him a smile.

"Today I make these vows to both of you—to be there for you, to stand beside you through the good and the bad, to be your light when it's dark, to be your comfort when it's cold, to be your rock when you need support. You and Grady are all that I'll ever need. Everything I have, everything I am, is yours." He places the gold wedding band on my ring finger.

Tears fill my eyes and I swallow, hoping like hell my voice will work.

"Chance." I pause, drawing in a breath. "I chose you all those years ago, and I never stopped loving you. You complete me in a way I can't describe, and today I invite you to share my life, our son's life. I—" I choke back a sob.

Chance squeezes my hand.

"I love you, Chance. I've always loved you. You are strong and compassionate and so pure of heart." I pause a moment as Mom hands me the wedding band. "I give you this ring as a symbol of our eternity together. You're my love, my light, my soul." I place the ring on Chance's finger. "Our love is never ending, like the circle of this ring."

Tears flow down my cheeks, but it's okay. I'm finished.

"Lovely," the officiant says. "I now pronounce all of you husband and wives. You may kiss!"

Chance grabs me, crushes his lips to mine.

And everyone else fades away as I kiss my husband for the first time.

BONUS CONTENT

Guess what? We've got some bonus content for you with Chance and Avery. Yup, there's more!

Click here to read!

A NOTE FROM HELEN

Dear Reader,

Thank you for reading *Broken*. If you want to find out about my current backlist and future releases, please visit my website, like my Facebook page, and join my mailing list. If you're a fan, please join my Facebook street team (Hardt & Soul) to help spread the word about my books. I regularly do awesome giveaways for my street team members.

If you enjoyed the story, please take the time to leave a review. I welcome all feedback.

I wish you all the best!

Helen

Sign up for my newsletter here:

http://www.helenhardt.com/signup

GET A FREE VANESSA VALE BOOK!

Join my mailing list to be the first to know of new releases, free books, special prices and other author giveaways.

http://freeromanceread.com

ALSO BY HELEN HARDT

Follow Me Series:

Follow Me Darkly

Follow Me Under

Follow Me Always

Darkly

Wolfes of Manhattan

Rebel

Recluse

Runaway

Rake

Reckoning

Billionaire Island (Wolfes continuation)

Escape

Gems of Wolfe Island (Wolfes continuation)

Moonstone

Raven

Garnet

Buck

Steel Brothers Saga:

Trilogy One—Talon and Jade

Craving

Obsession

Possession

Trilogy Two—Jonah and Melanie

Melt

Burn

Surrender

Trilogy Three—Ryan and Ruby

Shattered

Twisted

Unraveled

Trilogy Four—Bryce and Marjorie

Breathless

Ravenous

Insatiable

Trilogy Five—Brad and Daphne

Fate

Sex and the Season:

Lily and the Duke

Rose in Bloom

Lady Alexandra's Lover

Sophie's Voice

Temptation Saga:

Tempting Dusty

Teasing Annie

Taking Catie

Taming Angelina

Treasuring Amber

Trusting Sydney

Tantalizing Maria

Standalone Novels and Novellas

Reunited

Misadventures:

Misadventures of a Good Wife (with Meredith Wild)

Misadventures with a Rockstar

The Cougar Chronicles:

The Cowboy and the Cougar

Calendar Boy

Daughters of the Prairie:

The Outlaw's Angel

Lessons of the Heart

Song of the Raven

Collections:

Destination Desire

Her Two Lovers

Non-Fiction:

got style?

South

East

West

Bachelor Auction

Teach Me The Ropes

Hand Me The Reins

Back In The Saddle

Wolf Ranch

Rough

Wild

Feral

Savage

Fierce

Ruthless

Two Marks

Untamed

Tempted

Desired

Enticed

More Than A Cowboy

Strong & Steady

Rough & Ready

Wild Mountain Men

Mountain Darkness

Mountain Delights

Mountain Desire

Mountain Danger

Grade-A Beefcakes

Sir Loin of Beef

T-Bone

Tri-Tip

Porterhouse

Skirt Steak

Small Town Romance

Montana Fire

Montana Ice

Montana Heat

Montana Wild

Montana Mine

Steele Ranch

Spurred

Wrangled

Tangled

Hitched

Lassoed

Bridgewater County

Ride Me Dirty

Claim Me Hard

Take Me Fast

Hold Me Close

Make Me Yours

Kiss Me Crazy

Mail Order Bride of Slate Springs

A Wanton Woman

A Wild Woman

A Wicked Woman

Bridgewater Ménage

Their Runaway Bride

Their Kidnapped Bride

Their Wayward Bride

Their Captivated Bride

Their Treasured Bride

Their Christmas Bride

Their Reluctant Bride

Their Stolen Bride

Their Brazen Bride

Their Rebellious Bride

Their Reckless Bride

Bridgewater Brides World

Lenox Ranch Cowboys

Cowboys & Kisses

Spurs & Satin

Reins & Ribbons

Brands & Bows

Lassos & Lace

Montana Men

The Lawman

The Cowboy

The Outlaw

Standalones

Relentless

All Mine & Mine To Take

Bride Pact

Rough Love

Twice As Delicious

Flirting With The Law

Mistletoe Marriage

Man Candy - A Coloring Book

ABOUT HELEN HARDT

#1 *New York Times*, #1 *USA Today*, and #1 *Wall Street Journal* bestselling author Helen Hardt's passion for the written word began with the books her mother read to her at bedtime. She wrote her first story at age six and hasn't stopped since. In addition to being an award-winning author of romantic fiction, she's a mother, an attorney, a black belt in Taekwondo, a grammar geek, an appreciator of fine red wine, and a lover of Ben and Jerry's ice cream. She writes from her home in Colorado, where she lives with her family. Helen loves to hear from readers.

Please sign up for her newsletter here:
http://www.helenhardt.com/signup
Visit her here:
http://www.helenhardt.com

ABOUT VANESSA VALE

A USA Today bestseller, Vanessa Vale writes tempting romance with unapologetic bad boys who don't just fall in love, they fall hard. Her books have sold over one million copies. She lives in the American West where she's always finding inspiration for her next story. While she's not as skilled at social media as her kids, she loves to interact with readers.

vanessavaleauthor.com

facebook.com/vanessavaleauthor

twitter.com/iamvanessavale

instagram.com/vanessa_vale_author

amazon.com/Vanessa-Vale/e/B00PGB3AXC

bookbub.com/profile/vanessa-vale

tiktok.com/@vanessavaleauthor